The stories found in this book are horrible. I mean they're *real bad.*

Every author wishes to be read—sometimes even stories they wrote when they were worse at it than they are now need a little attention. That's what this book is for.

This is a collection of stories written over the span of thirty years. Some are bad. Some are not so bad. One is even based on a dream I had the night a famous author passed away. (That doesn't make it any less terrible.) I hope you enjoy them anyway.

TIPTOE THROUGH TIME AND SPACE

By K. J. Joyner

A COLLECTION OF FUNNY, SERIOUS, AND STRANGE TALES IN THE REALM OF SCIENCE FICTION AND FANTASY.

GODS HELP US ALL.

Tiptoe Through Time and Space
Joyner, K. J.

Published by the Writers of the Apocalypse
http://www.apocalypsewriters.com

Second edition
Cover assembled by Katrina Joyner
ISBN-13: 978-1-944322-41-0

TABLE OF CONTENTS

A CHANCE ENCOUNTER OF TWO

Black-eyed susans were Fox's favorite flower. The meadow was covered in their brilliant blossoms the day the dragon lumbered outside the cave to bask in the sunlight. Somewhere nearby a blue jay was singing proudly, and off in the distance was the gentle *clunk clunk* of metal banging merrily as some knight made his errant way through the mountains. All in all, it was a wonderful day to be alive.

And in love.

"For you, my love," Fire said, plucking a clawful of brilliant blossoms for Fox.

"Oh, they're lovely," Fox said, batting thick eyelashes and accepting them in a claw. "You're always so thoughtful. These will look lovely by the cave door."

The banging was louder now, but the dragon took no notice as he lolled happily amongst the blossoms. A bumblebee clumsily landed on his snout. Fox batted it away , and Fire snapped it up greedily. Yum.

"Do you hear that, my precious?" Fire said after he

managed to get the bumblebee's stinger out his mouth and the pain had finally begun to subside.

"Yes," Fox said, wincing at the dull ache. "It's a human, isn't it?"

"I think so," Fire said, regretfully rolling to stand on hind legs and survey the terrain. "We so rarely get bothered by humans anymore. Not since the accident. Do you think this one will want to play?"

"Oh, I do hope so," Fox said while wrapping a doting tail around Fire's neck. "Usually they run away screaming before I can even get the tea on the boil. Do mind your manners this time, dear. It would be nice to have someone over for dinner."

"Yes..." Fire's eyes narrowed as he orientated on the now obvious metal banging which was now accompanied by the clip-clop of equine hooves. "Dinner would be nice."

"I wonder if there are any mushrooms left from the last visitor," Fox mused just as the knight burst from the brush and into the meadow.

He was a mediocre sight as far as knights went. His shiny silver helmet contrasted sharply against his battered copper breastplate. His arms were bare except for a pair of oversized and obviously rusty gauntlets from which it appeared he had developed quite the nasty rash. Something vaguely resembling a feather hung limply from his helmet into his watery-blue eyes, which peered at the dragon from behind his nose guard. His horse, a half-starved gaunt creature with barely a tail to swat flies with, wuffled at the grass and took a large bite.

"Stand and deliver!" the knight cried, pointing dramatically. "Oh, damn! That wasn't right. Wait, be right back."

Bemused, the dragon cocked his head and watched the knight withdraw in order to re-emerge a second later.

"Advance and be recognized!" the knight cried, pointing again. The finger of his gauntlet drooped sadly.

"I think," said Fox helpfully, "you're supposed to say something like, 'Avant! Foul beast!' Although I could be wrong. That's what the last one said, isn't that right, Fire?"

Fire grunted.

The knight blinked, lowering his finger. "What?" he said, startled.

"Avant. You're supposed to say avant. And then we rush you. It's how the game goes. You've never played this before, have you?"

"Avant," the knight repeated, apparently shocked.

"Yes!" Fox clapped her claws together happily. "That's the way! Now, get out your pointy sword thingy and we'll fight. Oh, this is so much fun! You're supposed to wave it bravely and such before I actually come at you. How trained is your horse? Fire gets a little excited with the livestock, I'm sad to say."

"N-not very," the knight stammered, slowly fumbling

for the sword strapped to his back. It stuck halfway out of the sheath and refused to budge. The knight nearly fell from his horse as he tugged, pulled and grunted. The sword refused to move, gleaming rebelliously in the sunlight.

"Are you sure that's far enough?" Fire asked with a smirk. "Can we attack now?"

"Oh, not yet, dear," Fox said soothingly, patting Fire's arm with a gentle claw. "It's the boy's first time. Be nice."

"Do you need a little help?" Fox asked when it became apparent that the knight could not get his sword free. She lumbered a little closer, craning her head to examine the problem.

Forgetting the sword, the knight promptly yelled excitedly and kicked his horse into motion. The horse, more than eager to escape the dragon's clutches, promptly bolted. The knight, still grabbing for the reigns at the time, ended up flat on the grass with a loud clunk! Grasshoppers scattered out of the way.

"Oh dear," said Fox just as the knight moaned.

"He's down!" Fire said, leaping a bit in his excitement. "Let's eat!"

"Patience," Fox admonished. The knight tried to roll over on his side, but the armor was too heavy. The dragon knew that most knights kept other pet humans around in order to help out in such an emergency, but this human was very much alone. Poor bugger. A pang of pity stabbed her scaly heart when the knight started to desperately claw at the straps that held his armor on. "Let's help him," she said when the knight began to whimper. "Poor thing... Just look at him!"

"But, but," Fire protested.

Fox ignored her mate. Carefully, she edged as close as she could to the knight, who was weeping, and picked him up. He screamed and kicked wildly. "Stop struggling or I'll drop you," Fox said in her most maternal tone. She set the knight down on his feet and used the tip of her tail to brush off stray bits of grass from his armor. Stiffly, the knight stood there with his eyes squeezed shut. Fox gently removed the sword from its scabbard and offered it to the knight. "Would you like to try again? That was really a wonderful try for your first time. I think a bit of practice would work wonders for your sword arm."

The knight opened one eye slowly.

"Here," Fox said, still offering the sword. Fire grumbled unhappily, sending smoke plumes sailing to the sky as he fought to contain his fiery breath.

The knight screamed and ran.

"Now look at what you did!" Fox said to Fire. "You chased him away. I never get to play anymore!" With that, Fox went into the cave to sulk and would not come out again.

That evening, the horse returned to the meadow. Its

saddle was hanging on its underbelly; the knight had not buckled it on very well. It snorted in irritation, kicking occasionally at the bulky thing between its legs as it chewed grass. Fox took pity on it and, after casting a spell to keep it calm, removed the saddle and other gear. Then Fire had dinner. They put the tack by the cave mouth in order to return it to the knight, should he ever reappear. It made a lovely addition to the growing collection that was already there. The bones they stored in the back of the cave for a midnight snack.

The next morning, a loud shouting awakened Fire. "Avant, foul beast! Forsoothe! Come out and fight!"

Yawning, the dragon stretched first his wings then his claws. The shouting continued outside. After a minute, Fire poked his head outside of the cave to blink blearily in the sunlight. Standing just a few feet away was the knight, holding a pitchfork and looking even more terrified than before. "Who is it dear?" Fox said, waking. "Oh. It's the knight. Now, dear, pitchforks are for farmers. You're supposed to have a sword.... have you come to get it back? It's over there with the others." She gestured to a pile of swords nearby.

"You'll not fool me this time, dragon," the knight said, advancing a shaky step. "Old Myra told me about your dragon riddle tricks. Now, shut up and fight. Or die!" He jabbed Fire's toe with the pitchfork, which obligingly snapped.

"Ow," said Fox, snorting.

The knight, whose name was Kirk, swallowed as the dragon filled his vision with narrowing, yellow eyes. In truth, he was only an accountant for the local king. His father, a freeholder, had failed to pay taxes that year and was now sitting in jail. Kirk couldn't pay the debt on his meager salary, so when he heard of a local cattle-eating scourge, he decided to kill it. The reward on the beast's head was enough to pay back his father's debt while leaving him enough to purchase a small farm of his own. If he failed to kill the dragon, he would be dead. If he failed to pay his father's debt to the king, he would be jailed. Kirk knew where his priorities were on that situation.

Besides, there was also Lidea, the local witch's daughter; she of the golden hair, sparkling green eyes... And she was quiet enough not to annoy a man after a hard day's work. Secretly, Kirk hoped to impress her as well as the king. So he had borrowed an old sword, salvaged some armor from various forgotten rooms in the castle, and stolen a horse from a nearby farmer.

On his way out, he stopped to see Lidea one last time and ask the local witch for advice. Old Myra, the aforementioned local witch, said the bones thought success was possible... if he were brave enough.

Kirk knew nothing about being brave, but he knew desperation. Desperate was how one felt when a dragon narrowed an eye and said, chillingly, "Why, Fire, I believe this young scamp broke one of my nails. I just had them done last week, and now this one is chipped." Desperation was knowing your only weapon was a broken stick as a pile of perfectly good swords taunted you from just feet away.

People do strange things out of desperation. Kirk chose to throw the stick into the dragon's nearest eye and run for it. He did not stop running until he was on the far side of the meadow. Behind him, the dragon roared indignantly and shouted something about the price of having one's nails done.

Kirk stumbled to a stop. The dragon was still at the cave mouth, biting one claw distractedly while making strange moaning sounds to itself. Still glinting in the morning sun, the pile of swords beckoned. If he had been quick and brave enough, he could have grabbed one....

Well, before he was incinerated.

Maybe he could still get one while the dragon was distracted. His father was counting on him, the dungeon was waiting, and he would never be able to face Lidea again if he failed. He had no choice. He had to go back. Sighing heavily and praying a minute for the safe deliverance of his soul, Kirk resolutely made his way back to the cave mouth. The dragon was talking to itself again. That was probably the most disturbing aspect of this entire adventure.

"It doesn't look too bad, Fox," the dragon said as it extended one claw admirably. "It'll look better once they're all chewed to match." Suiting actions to words, Fire placed another toe into his snout and continued gnawing.

"It's terrible, Fire!" the dragon said, withdrawing the claw and sniffling. "They were so beautiful, and now they're ruined!"

"Don't look now, that knight is back again," Fire rumbled. The knight was advancing slowly, weaponless and apparently ready to die. Grudgingly, Fire had to admit this one little human had more nerve than most. Maybe Fox would let the knight stay on as a pet. At least, for a little while until Fire got hungry.

"I don't feel like playing right now," Fox said haughtily, averting her eyes so as not to look at the offending human. "Just take your toys and go home." Turning her back, she stalked partially into the cave. Fire turned around, saying, "Don't mind her, she's just fussy. If you really want to play, we still can. I'll even wait until you get your sword." With his tail, he plucked a sword from Fox's collection and dropped it at the knight's feet.

"I don't want to play," Fox grumped. "Send him home, Fire."

"No," Fire grumped back. "I like him."

"Well, I don't."

"Too bad."

"WHO ARE YOU TALKING TO?!?!" Kirk finally screamed, unable to take it anymore.

"Fire," said Fox. "Fox," said Fire. They answered together, and so the reply came out sounding like a garbled version of "Firefox," which was the dragon's name. Internally, the dragon considered it to be merely his "body name" that really did not apply to the two separate personalities residing within.

"Firefox...?" Kirk echoed. This dragon was surely possessed. He inched away a step, unsure of what to do. Then Kirk realized that he was falling into another one of the dragon's spells. If he did not shake it off, he would soon be scholar barbecue.

Swiftly, he picked the sword up and, with a wild yell, attacked. Sparks landed on his left boot when the sword's edge met the thick, metallic scales of the dragon's hide. A high and melodic pitch permeated the air as the blade vibrated. The motion jarred Kirk's arms and hurt his teeth. Nevertheless, he stepped back and brought the sword up for another try. The pitch turned into a soft ringing and did not stop. It was almost soothing.

The sword bounced on the second blow and sent Kirk staggering back a step. Before he could regain his balance, a sensuous tail wrapped itself around Kirk's waist and lifted him up. Kicking wildly, Kirk tried to slice the tail with the sword, which was now whining an eerie version of a local folk song. The tail was just as impervious as the rest of the dragon, it seemed. Each time he swung the sword, the musical pitch got louder. It was strange enough to be fighting a dragon that talked to itself, and now he had to deal with a singing sword. In the back of his mind, Kirk wondered if Myra had cursed him. He was going to die, he knew it. And maybe Lidea was really more talkative than she seemed, in fact she probably was a nag–

"It's not our fault, you know," Fox said conversationally.

"Not our fault at all," Fire joined with conviction. "It was an accident. Thorn did it."

"What makes you think it was Thorn's fault?" Fox said. "I think it was Bracka."

"Thorn," Fire accused stubbornly.

"It doesn't matter anyway," Fox said loftily. "What's done is done."

Unbeknownst to the dragon, Kirk was dwelling on his impending doom. Myra had told him to keep the beast talking and distracted. Dragons, according to the old witch, loved a good conversation and would do just about anything for a decent riddle. Keep it talking, the old witch had pounded into the boy's brain. Keep it talking. That was not as hard as he thought it was going to be. The problem, as best he could tell, was that the dragon would never talk to him.

"Are you saying," Kirk wheezed while thinking quickly, "someone did this to you?" The tail tightened bit by bit the more the dragon argued with itself. If this kept up, he would be pulp and the dragon would never realize it until the argument was settled. His fingers were going numb, and he dropped the sword. Thankfully, the song died as soon as it hit the dirt.

Those sagacious, yellow eyes orientated on the lad. "Oh, yes. Someone messed up a love spell, you know, and here we are. But Fire loves me, so I've nothing to complain about. We're happy, for the most part."

Fire rumbled something incomprehensible.

"Oh," said Kirk. "Yes. Well, you know, if you're happy then it really shouldn't matter whose fault it was. In fact, I'd be grateful. Perhaps. Urm. Sort of." The tail relaxed a bit, and Kirk took a deep breath before finishing with, "I suppose." He wished he had just packed his belongings and left the kingdom and wondered what he ever had seen in Lidea.

"What a sweet lad," Fox said to Fire before setting the gasping human on the ground. "I'm so glad he came to play." She batted her eyes at Kirk alluringly.

"I wonder why," Fire said.

"Oh, dear, do you think it's one of those cases? Little knight, you didn't just come up here to play, did you. Well, you can't have our treasure!" -which was a broken plate, a sad vase, and a collection of dried flowers the dragon had been giving to itself for a month straight —"But you've been so nice to us, and we've had so much fun, that I feel we've been friends forever."

"....thank you...." Kirk said weakly. This encounter had not gone at all as he had imagined it. The singing sword gleamed at his feet, but he felt no temptation to use it.

"I know!" Fox said with sudden inspiration. "You can have my entire sword collection! That odd one wasn't your sword anyway. Fire is just terrible at being able to tell the things apart. To tell the truth, I'm not sure which one was yours. There's any number of rusty swords in that pile, and I simply have no use for them. But your kind adores them, am I right? You can have them all as a friendship present. And then you can come back to play all you'd like!"

There had to be three dozen swords by the mouth of the cave. With that many, Kirk could sell them and buy his father's freedom. Providing the dragon actually allowed him to get away alive, he thought the gift very alluring.

This did not solve his dragon problem. The king expected results. With that still in the way, the dungeon would become his permanent home before he could blink.

When it came to occupants, the dungeon played no favorites. The rats down there were bigger than a small dog and twice as fierce. A week ago, the king had imprisoned a messenger from the neighboring kingdom, Uther, for daring to insinuate he had stolen their prize cattle. By the next morning, there was nothing left of the poor man except a shin bone.

When he petitioned the king for leave to slay the dragon, Kirk was warned that failure would not be tolerated. This dragon, the king said, must not be allowed to dine on another royal cow. At the time, Kirk figured that failure would result in death of some warm variety. Now he was faced with the prospect that failure could also be quite lucrative. The joke was not lost on him.

If only there were some way to keep the dragon away from the cattle herds, and himself, long enough for him to get his father, marry Lidea, and get out of the kingdom.

"Thank you ever so kindly," Kirk said, putting forward his best manners while his quick mind turned over the possibilities. "And perhaps, since we're such good friends, I might be able to ask your help with a little problem? This has been going on a while now, I fear, and I'm going to be in terrible trouble when I get home if something isn't done." Cautiously, he leaned forward and patted the end of the dragon's tail. It was cool to the touch and not slimy, as he had thought it would be.

Fox nearly shrieked in ecstasy. "ANYTHING for a friend!" Even Fire was overjoyed and nodded his head enthusiastically.

"It's just that," Kirk said delicately, stepping away a bit

and eyeing the widest escape route just in case, "something, and I'm not sure what, but something has been eating all my cows and sheep! Mind you, I don't mind, really I don't... I mean, everything has to eat... it's just that my lord doesn't feel that way." Dramatically, Kirk heaved a sigh. "I'm only a poor farmer, you understand, and not half as smart or noble as my king."

"Oh, he must be a wonderful person for you to say that," Fox said adoringly at her new friend.

"Yes, he is," Kirk stalled. "But, it's terrible the things he's put me through. He says its all my fault! And then he told me that if I didn't replace those cows and sheep, he'd kill me! That's why I'm here," Kirk placed a dramatic hand over his chest, "to learn how to fight the scourge! Everyone told me that you, er, liked…. To… play. I thought, if you'd play with me, then I could get better at fighting and win!"

"How horrible!" Fox gasped, recoiling. Fire snorted, flattered that he would be chosen to train a knight. Fox seemed to have not heard the rest of Kirk's statement. "What a nasty little man!" she continued. "Why, I'll fly down there and teach him a lesson—"

"NO!" Kirk cried, waving his hands in alarm. "I mean, that's not necessary. All I have to do is stop the rest of my cows and sheep from being eaten." Then, as inspiration finally began to strike, he said, "You don't know who has been eating them, do you?" He tried to look as innocent as he could.

"Yes, but if he's mean to you now, imagine how horrible he'll get in the future," Fox said, still a few sentences behind Kirk. "It's like the old one that lives in the mountains. Why, I swear old Raize is just getting impossible to deal with in his old age. No no, I've made up my mind. We'll level the castle at dawn."

"Please don't!" Kirk nearly sobbed, wondering if the neighboring kingdom of Uther would take him in. "He's... he's... really not that bad, and besides... he... uh... has ten children!" The king had two cats and a cousin.

"Oh!" Fox blinked and settled on her hind quarters. She apparently was rethinking the situation, much to the consternation of Fire who had just started to look forward to an old-fashioned castle burning. "Oh, dear. In that case... what can we do? Oh!" She blinked. "You mean to tell me that all those cows and sheep.... they're your cows? Oh dear. Oh dear oh dear. Fire, I told you to leave the vale alone!"

"I was hungry," Fire said defensively.

"There are plenty of wild deer and cows in the neighboring kingdoms," Fox said. "This knight is our friend! You don't want to get our friend killed, do you? After you ate his horse on top of it all?!?"

"You ate Mudd?" Kirk asked, genuinely hurt. Stealing that horse had been very difficult.

"But I was hungry," Fire whined.

"No matter, dear," Fox said consolingly to the human standing before her. "Maybe someone will give you a better horse for one of those swords over there. There's a lovely dagger, too, with pretty stones all over it. I think it belonged to an elf. I really can't remember."

Fire rumbled, feeling guilty.

"And I promise, from now on Fire will not even look at your cattle... unless you tell him he can. Isn't that right, Fire?"

The dragon nodded once before turning away, abashed.

"I... I don't know what to say," Kirk said. It was the truth, and he paused a minute. "Not that I ever thought it was you," he continued finally with fingers crossed, "but... thank you. I can tell my lord, and he'll be so happy he might even let me eat tonight!"

So pleased was Fox with her new friend's polite demeanor, she insisted right then and there that the knight stay for tea. Kirk demurred, saying he had to go home right away and tell his lord the wonderful news that their cows and sheep were safe at last. Privately, he knew this had been resolved too easily and was on guard for a surprise attack. Nothing happened, and soon Kirk gathered enough courage to ask if he could take his swords home now.

"Of course, dear," Fox said with a bat of her yellow eyes. "Fire, you help him. You ate his horse, after all."

Together, dragon and human felled a few saplings and

built a litter strong enough to carry at least part of the sword collection. Kirk loaded what he thought were the best ones on it and even stuck the Elvin dagger into his own belt. It was much too pretty to sell, and besides it didn't sing like the sword did. He whistled while he worked, happy for the first time that day and sure his troubles were over.

"There's just one other thing," Kirk said carefully to the dragon while they loaded the clumsy litter.

"What ever could it be?" Fox inquired, pausing to scratch her snout with a broadsword. She was allergic to humans, and her nose itched terribly. Any minute now, she would begin to sneeze uncontrollably.

"Well, without the cows, how will you eat?" Kirk said.

"Oh, how thoughtful!" Fox cried, nearly dropping the sword in her delight. "What a delightful human you are! But there's no need to worry. Fire and I will simply visit the neighboring vale and catch what we can. We can take care of ourselves."

"I'm sure you can, as capable and beautiful as you are," Kirk said in his most flattering tone. Fox batted her eyes and cooed. "You have been so kind to me, I would like to give you something. I thought perhaps I could give you some of the cows that I will be able to buy with these swords."

"How delightful!" Fox cried. Even Fire looked mildly

interested, although Kirk had no way of knowing that.

"I'll have them waiting for you in the vale in seven days," Kirk said. "I promise. You'll be able to tell they're mine because I'll mark them. Like this." With his dagger, he scratched a design in the earth.

"What a delightful design," Fox said. Once she began to use the word, everything was delightful. "Human, you are the most delightful creature I have ever met."" With that, they placed the final swords into the pile and she shooed the human away before her sneezes began to erupt. Fire considerately scratched her nose.

As he painfully dragged his cargo away, Kirk pondered a dragon's word and what it meant. Obviously, there was no way he could trust that dragon not to eat more livestock when it got hungry. However, with the money he stood to make from these swords he planned to buy a few cows. Then he hoped to hire the services of a nearby necromancer who specialized in various lethal potions. One bite of a poisoned cow, and that dragon would be dead meat. Then, oh happy day, there would be silence and the dragon would talk to itself no more.

In the meantime, the dragon would terrorize Uther's herds as they grazed in the neighboring vale. There would be plenty of time to set things up before the stupid beast figured things out. With luck, some hero would slay the dragon before it returned it's attentions his way.

Uther's king was very protective of his livestock. Uther's cattlemen raised the best in the land. Everyone knew it. The cattle were jealously protected. Once, Uther went to war simply because a neighboring ambassador had casually offered to buy a prized heifer.

If the dragon died in Uther at the hands of an avenging cowboy, Kirk's problem was solved. If the dragon returned to his own kingdom, Kirk need only point out it must be a different dragon. Did he not return triumphant with the dragon's hoard as proof? Then another hero could be sent to dispatch the dragon while Kirk found his necromancer to prepare the poison trap. It was perfect.

When Kirk was out of sight, Firefox settled down contentedly in the grass and resumed yesterday's activities. "For you," Fox said, handing Fire a flower. Life was certainly sweeter now that they had a new friend. Obviously, she could not show her affection by giving the knight flowers. The neighboring kingdom, however, had lots of fat, juicy cows and sheep. In fact, Uther prized the quality of their livestock so much that they branded each and every one for easy identification – marks that looked a lot like the one Kirk had drawn, come to think of it.

Oh well. She would just flit over there and grab a few to replace the ones Fire had so disrespectfully dispatched. After all, anything for a friend.

"He's such a nice lad," Fox said to Fire.

Fire grunted, chewing on his flower. "I suppose. I thought the elf was much more fun. He at least knew where our tender areas were." The dragon thumped his snout and belly triumphantly.

"Yes, but he didn't last nearly as long," Fox replied with a sigh. "Come to think of it, none of our friendships seem to survive before some catastrophe happens. Why just the other month, that nice princess we had died most mysteriously. I still say you were forgetting to feed her."

"At least we have each other," Fire said, echoing their earlier sentiments.

"Yes," Fox said, wrapping her tail lovingly around Fire's neck and stroking his eye-ridges. "I hope this one lasts a bit longer, though. We just haven't gotten to play as much as we used to since the accident."

THE GOLDEN SHIP

One night when I was a mere teenager, I had a dream about a golden clamshell ship that descended to the planet Earth centuries ago. I can still remember the hum in my dream, as well as the gleam of sunlight from the ship's faceted sides.

A golden clamshell, it descended slowly from the sky and hovered above the crashing waves near the cliff. Flashing jewels and candlelight flashed across its surface, keeping visual time with the sun. It hummed a melody slightly sour but with hints of a wonderful beauty.

Something opened near the top, and a woman stepped out. Platinum blond hair was captured by the ocean wind and whipped around a finely chiseled face. She grimaced, a pleasant expression to any but her own kind, and disappeared quickly within the golden vessel.

Gods, how she hated this miserable mud ball! If her ship did not need repairs so desperately, she would be on her way home to a well-earned vacation and quality time with her husbands. Having to take this detour to here of all places, just, it just, well, it made her so angry

She slammed doors behind her, grimaced again when the ship groaned, and sighed internally. Apologetically, she patted the framework and promised the ship that it would not be long. What they needed was right here and in great abundance.

Leisurely, she walked onto the bridge and closed the door carefully and lovingly behind her. She gave the wall another pat for good measure. Her small crew manned their stations and wisely ignored her. They had long ago grown accustomed to their captain's eccentric habits. Small disappointment gnawed at the captain: If just one of them would say something mutinous (even faintly), they could hurry out of there.

"Readings are growing erratic, Captain," said a young ensign. Display lights highlighted his fair face as sensors traced the outline of the ship and various components within.

"How much longer?" the captain asked as she studied the view screen, contemplating the world below. There was the cliffside , battered by the angry ocean waves. The forest ahead looked thicker than before, but she had been gone a long time by this world's reckoning. Things grew quickly here.

"Seven days at best," the youth answered cautiously.

The captain watched a while longer, then grimly sat in her chair.

"Very well," she sighed. "We'll mount an expedition after our midday meal." Closing her eyes and leaning back, she wished she could take a nap. There never was time for simple pleasures anymore. "I will need two volunteers," she said into the crew's silence, "or I can pick two recruits. Decide among yourselves, and be prepared after the meal."

Murmured *ayes* floated around her. A smile touched her lips briefly, flickering them down. They would obey. It was either that, or fix the ship themselves.

Ebher stood at the edge of the trees and looked long at the golden *thing* as it hovered and sang. The sun flashed from its surface and created a halo of light. It was altogether ethereal in a silent, somehow deadly sort of way.

He hoisted his kill, four rabbits and a squirrel, over his shoulder and turned to go. Poised in the shadows, he hesitated before turning back to the alien object. Curiosity warred against common sense. Should he go home and warn the others, or take a closer look?

Common sense won when he recalled his mother's urgent warnings: Avoid the cave, she had said the day before he, exploring, had disturbed a hibernating bear. Leave the wasps in peace, she had begged the morning before he was seriously stung for teasing them. He could almost hear what she would say now; Avoid that thing.

Ebher lived alone in a sheltered glade in the forest. It was not completely by choice. He was not altogether welcome in town. His face was lopsided, his arms gangly, and he towered over the tallest man. The children in town called him "Ebher the Giant Man." Others called him worse. He only went into town whenever he had no other choice.

"Our family has always been blighted," Grandmother would say as she swayed gently in her rocking chair. "My uncle Jaori was taken by the fae when I was small, and we've had trouble since. Just look you, even the cow cannae give a live birth. And when she does, it's striped all over. The little people beat the poor thing with sticks, says I, and those be the markings of it!"

As an impressionable child, Ebher doted on every word. Now, as an adult whose family had passed away long ago, he watched every stone for signs of the little folk. Offerings to them littered the landscape where he walked: saucers of milk, shiny stones, and the occasional bead.

He stepped into his yard and stopped. His front door was wide open. As every horrible tale his grandmother had ever told spun around in his mind, Ebher approached cautiously. Crouching down underneath his single window, he listened. Someone moved around inside, banging cups and scooting chairs around. Ebher put a hand to his chest, trying to still his beating heart.

"Ebher!" cried a high, familiar voice. He jumped, but smiled in relief. Poking out of the window a freckled face grinned down at him from beneath dangling wisps of copper-brown. "Quit yuir playin' around and come on inside! I brought carrots and leftover stew from last night."

Wilhelmina had come from afar with her mother years ago. Her father, she once said, had died in a foreign war. No mention was ever made of the rest of her family clan, if there were anyone at all. She would quickly change the subject if pressed.

Folk were friendlier to her than to Ebher, but there was alienation all the same. It was that in common which had founded their friendship. Kindnesses were traded daily in the form of rabbits, herbs, even blankets fresh off the loom.

If asked, Ebher would say that Wilhelmina was his only friend. Wilhelmina would say the same of Ebher.

"I see you brought somethin' home today," Wilhelmina said as she ladled steaming stew into a bowl on the table.

"Yah," Ebher mumbled, standing in his door and feeling altogether childish.

"Well, come then, sit!" Wilhelmina said impatiently. Her own bowl was brimming with stew, waiting. Ebher knew from experience that she hated her food cold, so he quickly stashed his kill in a corner and joined her. Wilhelmina was already praying over her food; A curious habit but one Ebher accepted.

It was a quiet meal, punctuated only with the sounds of eating. Wilhelmina, as always, finished first and leaned back in her chair. "So what did you see today, then?" she asked merrily.

Ebher stopped midchew. "Somethin' strange," said he. "A glowin' dragon, like in one of me grandmother's tales." Food forgotten, he looked at his ceiling and concentrated to recall the image. Something flickered behind Wilhelmina's eyes. Ebher missed it, or he would have known to stop. "T'looked like sunlight, or gold, and the sun couldna' capture it," he said wistfully. "There was someone ridin' it"

"Hush!" Wilhelmina cried.

"What?" Ebher asked, surprised. His eyes met the fire in hers and froze.

"Don't speak of them, it'll bring them!" Wilhelmina said in a hushed voice. "That be a daemon. It could trap yuir soul!"

His grandmother had spoken of goblins, gremlins, and kobolds digging their mines deep in the earth. Tiny winged beings danced in her words, or tall beautiful people living under the hill and holding court beneath the silver moon. Her world of tales could be terrible, or beautiful, but usually fair.

Not once had she spoken of daemons.

"I think," Ebher began.

"No!" Wilhelmina cried again, standing. "Don't let its beauty trick you! It'll take you, it will!" She was suddenly at his feet, hands clasped together and eyes closed. "Please, dear Lord," she begged of the ceiling, "send yuir angels to keep my Ebher safe!"

It was too much. Ebher scooted away from her. Wilhelmina looked at him and read the fear on his face. Tears filled her eyes. "Ach," she said in a strangled voice, "now I've made a fool of myself. But I won't have yuir soul taken by the devil!" She dashed out of the door before Ebher could think to stop her.

Next day, Ebher performed the unpleasant chore of going into the village to return the dishes. He would have gone anyway, he reminded himself, but that made it no easier. Devastation met his eyes as sandy streets, cleared away foliage, and waste being poured in the gutter. Dogs barked at him, announcing his presence to suspicious eyes. He preferred the clean forest and thanked the gods for his home there.

The children danced behind him and called him names. He hated that part the most: When he was reminded how awkward and ugly he was. Wilhelmina's pot was suddenly an uncomfortable weight in his hands. The dishes, awkward as they were, seemed too fragile to be trusted by him.

Wilhelmina lived with her mother at the edge of the village. Their cottage had once needed a new roof. Ebher had fixed that for them, and more. A tiny herb garden, sprinkled with late flowers, grew by the doorstep. New shutters slammed open as Wilhelmina's mother leaned out.

"She's not here," the old woman caroled across the yard. Ebher opened the door, a difficult feat with both hands full, and stepped inside.

"Not here?" he echoed dumbly. "Where is she then?"

"Don't know if she's not with you," the old woman said as she took the dishes. "Thought yuir place was where she went this mornin'."

"I'll find her," Ebher promised.

Wilhelmina's mother just smiled, unworried. "She's in th' Lord's hand," she said. "No harm will come to her." She continued to smile as Ebher left.

Strange woman, Ebher thought for the hundredth time as he followed the trail through the woods. Her daughter could be stranger, given the notion. But... when counted as the price for their friendship, overlooking their unique outlooks mattered nothing. He would do anything for Wilhelmina and her mother.

The cliff erupted suddenly from the trees. The golden thing hovered lower than the day before, but still was visible above the land. Ebher saw no trace of Wilhelmina. Ignoring it as best he could, he followed the trail to his house. He did not notice as three figures emerge from the golden object.

Ebher found Wilhelmina in his cottage. She flew into his arms, weeping loudly, and buried her face into his chest. Surprised by this sudden affection, Ebher forgot to ask her where she had been. Patting her back, he murmured soothingly.

"I thought the daemon had gotten you," Wilhelmina sobbed.

"I was lookin' for you," Ebher said. "I brought your dishes to your house, and you were gone."

Wilhelmina nodded in understanding. Then she laughed. "I'm bein' a silly girl," she exclaimed. Ebher was glad to see her tears turn into mirth, even if the embarrassed kind.

"Let me walk you home," Ebher said. "I know your mother doesn't usually worry, but she might be a worryin' this time."

Wilhelmina nodded, choking on sudden guilt, and together they walked back to the village. She was quiet on the way and submitted dejectedly. She barely said goodbye to him at her cottage door. Disturbed, Ebher made his way home. Leaves crunched under foot, reflecting his troubled thoughts.

Something flashed above him. Ebher looked up. Whatever it was, it circled just above the trees and lost altitude with each circuit. Fear hammered hard in his chest – it was an unfriendly fairy! He started to run, feet kicking up dirt in his wake. A high whine followed him through the brush.

Suddenly he was surrounded by...he could not imagine. He barely missed running into one as he skid to a halt on the trail, falling to his bottom and jamming his elbows. It was horrible, and wondrous, and strange all at once.

He could only think of them as silver chariots, each floating through the air with no horse to pull it as harnessing the wind. A woman, dressed in nothing more than a wisp of cloth dyed with a pattern of golden-green leaves, guided one with two reins of thick metal. Two other chariots, mastered by tall men with bulging muscles, cut Ebher's escape from behind.

Ebher whimpered softly when the woman settled her chariot to the ground. The men bristled where they hovered nearby. Ebher and the woman exchanged a long look; measuring on her part and open-mouthed on his.

"Greetings," the woman said slowly, halting over the syllables. Her accent, stranger than Wilhelmina's, fluted through the word and made it into music.

"Hello," Ebher responded faintly after a space of expectant silence. He waited for his death, knowing it was coming, wondered why it had not happened. His grandmother's cackle echoed somewhere in the past.

The woman smiled a tiny smile. "What is your name?" she asked hauntingly.

"Ebher," he mumbled into his chest.

"Ebher," she repeated. Again she smiled, wider and encouraging.

"I know who you are," Ebher said with faint bravery. "You're Titania, Queen of the Fae Folk."

"Last I was here," the queen mused half to herself, "I was chieftess of the Star Clan...What, I wonder, has made such a drastic change? Have your people changed that much in so short a time?" Her silver-blue eyes snapped from their reverie and back to Ebher. "What are you?" she demanded imperiously.

Ebher shrugged, looking down and remembering his ungainly appearance. "Just Ebher," he muttered.

"Perhaps you could be more," the woman said. "We could discuss the possibilities, you and I."

Like a shout, his mother's voice resounded from the past. "Stay away!" Images of his grandmother, cackling and rocking by the fire, accompanied details of her stories: The family blighted. Their sickly cow. Uncle Jaori, taken by the fae long before Ebher's birth.

Rather than arouse fairy wrath with outright rejection, Ebher continued to look down in silence. He was dimly aware that she was holding a hand out to him, but he pretended not to see.

After a while, the woman lowered her hand. Her smile did not fade. "Another time then," she said. "Perhaps?"

"Per'aps," Ebher managed to say.

"We will see each other again," she promised. Her chariot floated her up and back into the air. Her guards followed without hesitation. Ebher was left with no evidence of his encounter.

Evening fell like a cloudless dream. Stars winked to life one by one overhead. The captain sat on the cliff's edge and alternately watched the sea and stars. Great was her comfort as she gazed at them, contemplating her next move. They were the only things constant in this world where everything else grew old and died with just fifty-odd solar revolutions.

"You'll never get one if you keep making faces at them like that," her second in command said from the shadows. He approached her without fear, unlike most of the crew.

"It couldn't be helped," the captain replied with a sigh. "He smelled like rotten fish dried in the sun. Won't these creatures ever learn to bathe?"

"He doesn't need to be especially clean anyway," her second said. "So long as he's healthy."

"A fine specimen," she said. "Stronger than most, I dare say. We'll get him. Faces or no."

Her companion snorted with mirth. "Even yours."

The captain refused to be baited. "Watch them when they're among their own," she said philosophically. "They bare their teeth constantly, growling and spitting in their pathetic excuse for a language. So very animalistic."

"They are barbarians," was the casual remark.

The crash of the waves coupled with the sick humming of the ship were the only sounds for a brief space of time. The captain turned toward her vessel worriedly. "It's getting worse. We have a couple of days, at best, before we're stranded here."

Her second said nothing. What had to be done was obvious and needed no discussion. The stars twinkled overhead, but only the captain and her crew knew for certain whether they continued to do so after the sun created the new day.

Ebher might have gone to see Wilhelmina, but the muted terror of his encounter kept him indoors. He passed the time by mending his clumsily made furniture. The sun passed its zenith and began the slow journey down.

Someone knocked loudly at his door. Ebher, gingerly testing a chair, jumped in alarm. The chair collapsed underneath him.

Rubbing his sore posterior, Ebher approached the door. The knocking had stopped, but Ebher knew his guest waited impatiently on the other side. His heart skipped as fear resurfaced its ugly head. Squeezing his eyes shut, he opened the door a crack and said, "Yes?"

"Ebher!" cried Wilhelmina's bright voice, full of

amusement and tugging his eyelids open. "You look daft, standing there with yuir eyes closed like a child hidin' under th' covers!" She giggled, belatedly smothering it into her sleeve.

She had been picking autumn flowers. Each plait of her hair was adorned with their soft petals. Regarding him with the mysterious secrets of womanhood, her eyes reflected the leaves adorning her hair. Sweeping by him and into the house, she left the soft scent of her prizes behind.

Not as beautiful as Titania, Ebher thought guiltily. Still, there was a certain wild charm about her as she held up her basket for his inspection.

"I brought honey cakes," she said with great satisfaction.

If Titania herself were to have burst through Ebher's door, he would not have stopped smiling. Ebher's favorite thing in the entire world was honey cakes.

She watched him devour two pieces before delicately taking one of her own. From around a mouthful, she said, "I'm terribly sorry about yesterday. I know I can be a goose sometimes."

Ebher thought about his encounter in the forest and said nothing. There was no way he could tell her about it, not without exciting her again. Her fear of the golden thing was not entirely unfounded, and he almost did get taken away.

"What's th' matter?" Wilhelmina asked, touching his arm.

"Nothin'," Ebher managed to say after laboriously swallowing. "I just remembered somethin' I have to do."

"Oh." Wilhelmina set her basket onto the table. "You have ta check yuir traps, I suppose? With winter comin' an all."

Ebher nodded, feeling terribly guilty.

"I'll just leave the basket here then. You can bring it to me later."

"Yes."

"I suppose I should be goin' home now."

"Um, yes. I suppose."

"Perhaps I'll see you tomorrow?"

"Yes."

Wilhelmina gave Ebher a long, strange look before leaving.

It was true there were traps to check, Ebher thought to himself as he shuffled outside. Winter would soon be at hand, and his stores were not as fat as they should be. He shuffled from trap to trap, but they were empty aside from one scrawny rabbit. Surely there was no harm in setting out more snares near the cliff. He could look at the golden dragon, or whatever it was, in the process, and no one would be the wiser.

Deep within, his mother's warnings buzzed like angry

hornets. Ignoring them, he made his stealthy way to the cliff. With the setting sun flashing from the thing's surface, his mother's warnings became a low mumble, then a whisper, silence.

Ebher, left alone with only his unreliable curiosity, stared silently at the hovering thing.

"Beautiful, is he not?" a sultry voice said from nearby.

Ebher jumped, a frightened beast, and turned. The fairy woman, as if from thin air, half grinned as she stepped toward him. She was alone.

"I said do you think he is beautiful?" she asked again.

Ebher swallowed, regretting his meal as it threatened to leave his stomach. He nodded obediently. Encouraged, the fairy reached for Ebher's hand. When he did not respond, she only nodded and gestured toward the thing.

"Even I, having seen him every day for the past seventy years, must admit he is a sight to behold."

"What is it?" Ebher asked in a hushed whisper. He tensed, expecting a painful rebuke, and was astonished when his ethereal visitor smiled wider.

"A ship," she said. "My ship. His name is *Sleewagh*. Would you like to take a closer look?"

Had Ebher shaken his head harder, it would have fallen off. The fairy laughed, a high sound reflecting the joyful cry of small birds. Ebher was astonished that she was not insulted by his noncompliance.

"I like you," the fairy said. "You have a mind of your own. You are different from others I have met of your kind."

"Others?" Ebher asked sharply, thinking of the uncle he had never met. "Is it true that they are still there, under your spell to remain young forever with you?"

The expression she gave him was unfamiliar. "Oh, are they saying that now?" she asked softly, curiously, and somehow more to herself than him. "Truer to the mark, I suppose..." Again, her attention returned to Ebher as if traveling from very far away. "It might comfort you to know they all came willingly, and they are alive. Waiting."

"For what?" Getting bold, he dared to look her into the eyes. She seemed not to return his stare, but looked behind him.

"For someone like you," was her easy reply. She laughed again at his shock. "So hard to believe? Know that when I and my people come to this place, it is only to find someone like you. Willingly. I take them aboard *Sleewagh* and ride away, and only return when I must."

"What becomes of those you take?" Ebher heard himself say. "Do they live as slaves? Are they dead? Killed?" A large lump took root in his throat. If they had come for someone like himself, and here he was, what happened next?

"Shush," she said soothingly when he stepped away

from her. "Willingly is what I said. Would you call some-one who served you willingly a slave?"

Unsure, Ebher kept silent.

"We need you," the woman said, ignoring his shuffling feet and downcast glances.

"I'm sorry," Ebher said, edging even farther away.

"Consider us at least?" Her voice ended on a hopeful note. Pity moved Ebher long enough to make him pause a few minutes "Imagine, for a moment, the fantastical places you will go. You will ride among the stars, immortal. And beautiful."

Ebher turned and ran as fast as he could for the safety of his house. The fairy did not try to follow.

Evening, settling cool and calm over the land, brought fear with it. He tried to ignore it as he shuffled in his home, trying to find things to do. Too soon, the supply of chores was exhausted.

Boredom, however, was an easy thing for Ebher to de-feat. He made himself comfortable by the fireplace, took out his knife and a carefully selected piece of wood. Some-times he could let his mind wander on these occasions. It felt good, to be able to let his life go for a while.

A beautiful face, he decided as gouged shavings fell to the floor. The nose curved, like so. Pouting lips, with a tendency to smile, took shape quickly under Ebher's ad-ministrations. He started to carve her eyes.

Something bumped against his door. Ebher froze, a statue carving a statue, and listened. Not even the crickets sang, marking the silence and waiting. Nothing moved.

His concentration was broken. On shaky legs, Ebher crossed the single room in his cottage and buried himself in the furs of his bed. He stayed there until morning.

"Do something!" the captain snapped. The mechanic, an ensign on her first assignment, cowered and darted furtive glances to a platform on the ship's hull.

"We could capture a lower life form," the ensign offered. "It would last us a day or two. But we can't keep doing that."

The captain said nothing, merely continued to pierce the young woman with her steely eyes.

"The ship," the ensign stammered. "The ship might be damaged if the delay lasts any longer."

The captain knew that. Despair dampened her temper. She released the ensign from her gaze and looked toward the forest. "We will not be stranded here," she said with feeling. "I swear it."

Again Ebher crouched behind a tree and watched the golden dragon. Patience was his strongest virtue; he had been hiding there for hours. The fairies were busy around their golden vessal. Each of them were enviously perfect in proportion with golden hair that sparkled like gold in the sunlight. They crawled on the beast's hide or rode their strange chariots as they each found something to do. Titania stood on her own chariot in the air nearby and gave orders as she saw fit.

In his hands, Ebher fingered a shirt. The fabric, which looked heavy and hot, was light as air and just as cool. It shimmered in the shadows with a life of its own. Ebher did not want to touch it, but he was afraid it would disappear if he let it go.

He had found it outside his door that morning. It was an fairy thing, something from *her*. A gift, he supposed as he looked at the thing, to woo him.

Why him? He looked at those perfect and magical people and knew he could never hope to be like them, or to fit in with them, or dare to compare to them. His own people had rejected him because of his misshapen looks. How could they be any different? No one wanted him around. Except for Wilhelmina.

If Wilhelmina saw the golden creature, she would panic and demand that it be burned. Ebher had not seen Wilhelmina since the last time. He still had her basket. It should be returned, he knew that, but somehow things seemed unimportant in the face of the golden dragon.

Ebher shifted position, straining to see better. Two men, hauling a struggling calf, approached the queen and knelt.

Titania's smile made Ebher's heart pound as she pointed to the dragon. The calf was hauled in that direction – to feed the dragon, he assumed.

It was now or never, while they fed the golden thing. Ebher crept forward, into the open, and further still over the turf. Unobserved, he lay the shimmering shirt on the ground and spread it neatly. Then he turned and went back into the bushes, behind the trees, to obscurity. The returned gift flashed in the sun, bound to attract attention. Ebher left.

Knocking, insistent and loud, battered its way into Ebher's dreams. He groaned as he struggled to stand, wrapping a fur around himself and lighting a lamp.

Wilhelmina needed to visit at a more convenient time, he thought as he staggered to the door. She could wait for that basket. Was it morning, or evening?

What met his sleepy gaze caused him to shout and slam the door shut. He leaned against the wood, trembling. The lamp fell from his fingers and extinguished itself.

"Ebher," fluted a familiar voice from outside, "isn't this a breach of your people's hospitality? To leave me standing out here in the chilly air?"

That was fine with Ebher, but he croaked, "I'm sorry." It was all he could think to say. What did you say to a fairy standing on your doorstep in the middle of the night?

"Please," Titania said. "Ebher, let me in. I promise no

harm will come to you tonight. And I shall be gone by to-morrow."

Promises by the other kind, his grandmother had said, were binding but tricky. It was wisest not to deal with them at all, but if necessary then one had to be careful. One little phrase could be twisted until what you thought promised was wrong.

Sometimes dead wrong.

Still, there was nothing wrong with letting her in. She did promise that no harm would come to him tonight. She would be leaving the next day, so she would not be around to harm him then either.

Ebher cracked the door. Titania stood in the moonlight, looking like the goddess herself. The door opened wider.

"So wise," Titania said graciously as she stepped across the threshold. Ebher followed her with his eyes while he relit the lamp and held it out like a shield. She looked at it curiously before saying, "How very clever. There were on-ly tallow candles the last time I was here."

Wilhelmina's basket, laden with dried fruit and meats, was the next object of curious scrutiny. The queen held it in her delicate hands and sniffed. "Do you eat this stuff?" she asked incredulously. "Ghastly."

"I'm sure," Ebher mumbled shyly, "that things in your slwagh are much finer. Being magic and all."

"*Sleewagh,*" she corrected with a trace of annoyance.

"Sorry," Ebher said, studying his toes.

"Oh, your house does have its own charm." She stepped toward Ebher. Ebher backed away until he bumped into the door. "Do not be frightened."

Ebher would try, but he could make no promises.

"I came to speak to you about *Sleewagh*." She turned, spotted his chair by the fireplace, and confiscated it. "It is an honor I offer you," she continued. "In my time, only thirty-three have been chosen." Her eyes turned inward, not truly seeing the glowing coals in the fireplace, and she muttered, "Now, the old captain let the poor ship suffer. Only seventeen, mostly lower forms. *Sleewagh* has truly flourished since I disposed of that"

"Lady?"

Her eyes snapped back to attention. For an instant, they burned with a cold intensity. "Ebher," she said. "Do not you want to be a hero?"

Embarrassed silence.

"Ah well," the woman said. She smiled. "Look just outside the door. I have brought a gift for you. One that I don't think you will want to refuse."

The rebuke in her voice pushed Ebher into obedience. "A bottle?" he asked foolishly. He picked it up.

"Wine," said she, beckoning for Ebher to approach. "Not very old, but again..." She sighed. "Nothing here is."

Rustling in the bushes. Someone cursed in a high, complicated trill of syllables.

"Be quiet, idiot!" the captain's second hissed.

"Apologies," whispered the first voice. "It's these thorns." More rustling. Two shadows carefully detached themselves from the overcrowded bush to find new darknesses.

"Better," said the second in command. "Now the waiting will be more tolerable."

The other only curled his lips in his people's upward expression of loathing. He hated this waiting, this entire business, almost as much as he hated the captain. Kidnapping, he had often suggested, was the easiest way to solve the problem.

It was a suggestion the captain constantly vetoed. She liked to do things her way, and anyone who did not agree could find another way home. Or take the subcreature's place.

The bottle reflected the fire and sloshed a deep tone, suggesting emptiness. Ebher sat slumped against his chair, where the fairy still sat, and gazed at the world through drooping eyelids. He had only taken a single sip, but that was usually all it took. He was smiling to himself.

"We are a desperate people," the queen was saying urgently. "Our own men are not as strong as you. Nor half as brave. That is why we always pick one of your people over our own."

"But," Ebher said against the struggle to speak clearly, "what would I ha' to do?"

"You would travel with us," was the reply. "Protect us in need, even guide us when the time comes." The fairy tenderly stroked Ebher's hair; hesitantly at first, as if the mere touch filled her with dread. "And you would always be with me."

He turned, giving her a look of worship. "Always?"

"So long as I am queen." Her smile faded a little. Through the frown that followed, Ebher felt like she was trying to put on a pleasing expression. When the smile returned, it dazzled him.

"I dunno," Ebher said. "There's much I gotta do here."

"Oh?" She withdrew her hand. "Do you have family?"

"A frien'."

"Friend?" Her inquisitiveness cut like knives. "Just a friend?"

"Special frien'." Ebher leaned forward, unsteadily, and picked up his woodcarving from its spot by the fireplace. "Wilhelmina. Makin' this for her."

Titania took the carving and admired it. "Beautiful," she said with genuine awe. "It looks like me."

Ebher only shrugged. He did not always choose the results of his carving. Wood, he always said, had its own spirit. Perhaps this one wanted to reflect the queen.

"Do you want to mate with this friend, then?" The carving was dismissed, set on the floor beside its creator.

"Just a frien'." Never more than that, he thought with unfamiliar bitterness. He was too ugly, and she...

"I see." Titania shook her head. "You have a serious problem."

"I know."

"What a pity you don't look like the rest of them, eh? Or better yet, like one of my kind. Bet she'd look twice at you then." A large tear trickled past Ebher's nose. A perfect fingertip brushed it away. "I can do that for you, Ebher." The fairy's voice had become intense. "In return for helping me, I can give you physical perfection."

It was almost impossible to think past the wine-induced haze over his mind. "No lie?" he managed finally, after trying unsuccessfully to believe her for a few minutes.

"Of course not," the queen said. She leaned down to him, boring him with her eyes and tantalizing him with the breath of her lips. "Remember, Ebher, what I am. There are many things I can do, or at least have done."

Perhaps it was her perseverance that wore him down. Or her words promising grace, beauty, and acceptance. Or the wine. Something touched Ebher that night and robbed him of his mother's voice of reason. Before he collapsed gently to the floor, he swore to Titania that he would go with her.

The captain stepped over Ebher's inert form and glided to the door. Opening it wide, she gestured into the darkness. Her second in command was the first to the house. His companion, and their two guards, were only steps behind.

"We have it."

Everyone smiled with relief. They did not think the ship could hold out more than another day.

"But first," the captain said, raising a finger of warning, "the good doctor here must do a service for me."

"As always," the doctor, still picking thorns from his sleeves, said with a sneer. "What is it this time?"

The captain measured the man in a swift glance and filed the memory away for future reference. His insubordinance could be taken care of next time the ship needed repair. "Do you see this misshapen lump?" she asked, prodding Ebher with a toe. "I want you to change it. Sculpt it into something pleasing."

"Why bother?" the second in command asked. The doctor was already gathering his tools from their hiding place outside.

"Because I am a woman of my word," the captain said. "I want him to see that."

Daylight. The ship hung even lower by the cliffside and

did not hum so much as whine. Two concerned mechanics took readings and hovered near the upper platform. All else was quiet with the peace of morning.

The silver chariots burst from the trees suddenly, gliding close to the ground in perfect formation. The first four, driven by a solitary passenger, skimmed in a business-like manner past tree branches and rocks. The second in command, leading the party, held his head high, and he was smiling. The doctor also looked relatively pleased.

The last vehicle, laden with two passengers, flew lower than the others. Titania controlled it with unbound hair whipping in her companion's face and her lips curled in a grimace. The mechanics were alarmed at first sight of it, but remembered past triumphs and nodded to each other.

The riders settled on the grass and stepped down. Titania's companion was revealed.

It was Ebher, but no one would have recognized him. He stood as straight as a young sapling. His hair flowed around his shoulders like glass. His smile was perfection in a chiseled face. Only his eyes were not changed, but even they looked at the world with a difference.

"Come," Titania said, taking his hand.

Approaching the ship closer than he had ever imagined, Ebher did not balk or shy away. Clambering behind his fairy queen, he made it to the platform and stood at her command. He stared into her face and continued to smile.

Two ensigns gingerly bound his wrists to the ship and stepped back. The captain looked at him for a long while.

"My hero," she said, mockingly. Ebher's smile was empty of thought or freewill. The doctor had done his job very well.

She disappeared into the ship behind the others and closed the door tightly. Something inside the ship went *clung* and it shuddered. The whining changed its pitch and grew louder. The air vibrated with the new song.

Ebher remained as he was, looking at the sky and smiling. A light began to pour around him, enveloping him in a myriad of color. At first Ebher was an immobile statue within this rainbow. Then his knees buckled beneath him and he sagged against the bonds. Realization dawned in his eyes, his smile faded. He wondered if he were traveling the rainbow, and would he meet a leprechaun there. He caught sight of his perfect hands, bound as they were, and the smile returned. Titania had kept her promise.

Something at the edge of the trees wailed.

"Systems are up," the ensign said excitedly. Everyone was clustered behind him to watch the ship's scan diameter monitor every ounce of energy being fusioned with the ship. They knew that outside, the human's particles were being systematically scattered and brought into the ship's fuel lines to be processed when needed.

"Good," whispered the captain, very pleased. Ebher was stronger than she had thought. The power continued to flow unabated. By the look of things, they would have enough energy to make three trips home and back with plenty to spare. "We're going home," she announced.

Wilhelmina ran toward the golden thing. She cried Ebher's name as she went. The man on the platform, she was sure it was Ebher but it was hard to tell with the light, did not notice. He was looking at his hands and legs as if he had never seen them before.

She stood at the edge of the cliff and looked up, shading her eyes against the combination of sun and ship. Her face was wet with tears. She held up the little carving.

The ship's song was now pure beauty. Wilhelmina cursed its evil and her own futility. She prayed that they would let Ebher go. However fervent the wish, it could not be heard over the thrum of new life.

The light went out from the empty platform.

The captain gave the order. Without warning, the ship took off, streaking across the sky and into the clouds. Wilhelmina stood alone with only the carving for company.

She let her self-pity mingle with the ocean below. Slowly the normal sounds of life, unheard for days, returned around her. The carving's beautiful face mocked her with its half smile. Wilhelmina threw it into the water.

Wiping her eyes, she turned toward home. Her mother would grieve, but not as much as she. Grieving was all they could do. That, and pray for mercy.

Mercy on the soul of Ebher, beguiled by beauty.

LIVING

Somewhere near the dawn of time, there sits an old woman with snow white hair and gray-filmed eyes. She sits on the hilltop where the cool winds blow, and she feels the sunshine on her wrinkled, freckled skin. She can't see it anymore, but she knows the sun is yellow in its heated glory, and she smiles in its direction. Wisps of wintry hair play around her ancient face, reminiscent of the beauty that once was.

You probably wonder who she is, this ancient relic. Sometimes, she wonders, too. She knows who she used to be, though, and has learned to answer the calls of those around her. She has worn many labels through the years, all fitting perfectly one way or the other. In this moment, she is only aware of her universe.

A child clambers on the hills, his knees dirty and small, brown hands clutching a bedraggled bouquet of flowers. "Gramma!" he calls, waving madly. The old woman turns her face in his direction, chuckling softly. She doesn't need her sight to know what the child's appearance represents, having been a mother in her own time.

The boy presses the flowers carefully into his grandmother's hands, mindful that they do not drop into her lap. She smells them, and with the scent her mind fills with colorful images of petals long gone. It is a good moment, and she relishes it. The boy smells them, too, but is soon distracted by a wandering flutterby.

As he scampers off, the old woman lays into the soft grass and closes her eyes. The sun is warm on her face, and the earth cradles her like Mother's embrace. She can hear the boy approaching, and something tickles her nose.

The boy giggles, hopping away and dropping his new-found feather. Grandmother laughs, and in one swift movement grabs the child before he can get away. She has had much practice through the years, and tumbles the boy into her arms like a pro. She hugs him, and he her. The sun warms them both, but not as much as the feeling they are sharing between each other.

It is a good day to be alive.

A TROLL'S TAIL

This story is a spin-off from my first novel, Black Wolf, Silver Fox.

Finnbhear, don't go too far!" his mother called from the door of their little stone house. Her embroidered green skirts flared around her, leaves whipped by the summer winds.

"I won't," Finnbhear called sulkily, gamboling away fast as he could. He hated when his mother did that. He was grown now, past thirteen summers, and needed no protecting.

He sought out his favorite haunt, a hollow tree with large gnarled roots by a stream. The cool darkness of the tree's innards lent a feeling of peace. Finnbhear curled into the corner, sulking with intent to stay forever.

There was no telling how long he had been there. It might have been hours before the youth lifted his head to listen. Something or someone was nearby, shuffling the forest floor with loud sweeps.

Finnbhear reached for the small knife at his waist. It was a child's toy, but had to be enough. Warily, he peeked out.

"Finnbhear!" someone cried, leaping into his face. Finnbhear yelled, scooting back with his knife held in front. His perpetrator grinned.

"Kegal, you fell-born, vindictive wight!" Finnbhear cried, relishing his curses. His mother would have slapped his cheek for it, but she was not there.

"Got you that time," the vindictive wight chuckled, squatting on his haunches. He was a skinny lad that preferred ragged brown breeches and bare feet. His freckled nose wrinkled with mirth.

"I'll get you," Finnbhear growled, rushing out. The boys tumbled over each other, laughing, as each tried to best the other. It was Finnbhear who won, as usual, with a clever twist of the other's arm.

"'T hurts!" Kegal cried, face in the dirt, kicking his legs. "Let me go!"

"What'll you give me?" Finnbhear demanded, giving the other's arm an extra twist.

"Ow! Me mother's hawthorn branch! OW! Diamonds from the troll's hole! Owww! Three times I ask, let me go!"

Finnbhear mercilessly held his grip. "Apologize for scaring me," he said with a wicked grin.

"No!" Kegal exclaimed. Then, "Oww-ohhh! All right!

Just let me go!"

Finnbhear released the other. Kegal bounced up, rubbing his arms and glaring. He kicked a clump of leaves.

"Say it," Finnbhear prompted, crossing his arms. His father often did that when being stern. The gesture made Finnbhear feel very adult.

"No," Kegal said, skipping away with a flurry of leaves.

Finnbhear sighed, standing to brush his clothes off. Always, it was the same. He could have diamonds, sacred hawthorn, but never an apology. At his age, it was not riches or luxury Finnbhear coveted. It was the unattainable.

Kegal produced a silver flute from somewhere in his rags and started to play. He sat on a fallen log with his eyes closed, at one with his music. Finnbhear knew a stab of envy.

"You promised to teach me to play," he said.

Kegal broke off his song to regard his friend. "So I did," he said. "But if you want that today, you'll ask properly."

Blowing out through his nose, Finnbhear considered. He hated playing word games with Kegal. The brown lad liked to change the rules, usually in the middle of the game.

But, Finnbhear truly wanted to play the flute.

"Seven times I ask," Finnbhear said finally. "After that, no more."

With surprisingly no fuss, Kegal handed the flute to

Finnbhear. Finnbhear gingerly took the instrument, placed it to his lips and blew. The note fell flat, like squashed lettuce.

"You sound like a scared goose," Kegal laughed.

"Do not," Finnbhear retorted before trying again.

"You'll play no fair courts," Kegal said with a shake of his head. "Unless you play the mortal realm. They think anything sounds pleasant."

At the mention of mortals, Finnbhear lowered the flute. "Might we go to the human realm someday?" he asked eagerly. "I've always wanted to see a mortal. I know you can take me."

The thought of people who survived totally without magic fascinated Finnbhear.

"Just like an elf," Kegal sneered. "You're practically a mortal yourself. Just look in the water at your own reflection!"

"Am not a mortal," Finnbhear said stoutly. "My ancestress was a wood nymph. Her husband was a Danaan." This last bit he added proudly.

"So you claim," Kegal said. "But ye live in a house, not a tree. Just like a human."

"Take it back!" Finnbhear cried.

"Shan't."

This time, the boys wrestled in earnest. When they finally parted, both sported bloody noses and various scrapes. A large bruise was beginning to discolor Kegal's cheek.

"You're in an ill mood," the lad muttered, rubbing his cheek and eyeing his friend warily.

Instantly sorry, Finnbhear flopped down on the ground. It was true, he was in a bad mood. His father had gone to fight in a skirmish, common between the local chieftains. Two months ago, with the dispute settled, his neighbors had returned. But not Angus, his father.

Just past thirteen, bordering manhood, and now he was fatherless. Finnbhear fought against the ache inside him. He tried not to blame his father. Tried not to feel.

Kegal said, "T'must be hard, losing your father," as if reading Finnbhear's mind.

"Haven't you lost kinsfolk before?" Finnbhear spit.

"Nay," was Kegal's reply. "I left my family long ago to become this." He grabbed a fistful of rags and yanked happily.

"I wish I could do that," Finnbhear said wistfully, looking up at the treetops. "We could play all day long and never have to worry about anything. Wouldn't it be grand?"

Bounding, Kegal was at Finnbhear's side in an instant. "Why couldn't you?" he asked. "Hai, you could be my brother!"

Finnbhear sat in wonderment. "You could make me a fairy?"

Kegal looked sly. "P'raps," he murmured. "But you'd have to face a test."

"I can do it." Finnbhear hit his chest with a fist. "I'm stronger even than Uncle Bhinn." He neglected to mention that his uncle was an invalid with the wasting disease.

"Follow me, then." Kegal struck off, heading south. Finnbhear scrambled to follow, getting slapped in the face by branches. The wight never paused to consider his struggling friend.

Hundreds of scratches later, they arrived at a thicket of thorns. Kegal crawled right in. Finnbhear hesitated.

"Come on," Kegal hissed from within the bush.

"There's no easier way?" Finnbhear asked, looking around.

"Not if you want to be my brother," Kegal retorted.

Finnbhear got on all fours. "This had better not be a trick," he warned. He pushed, headfirst, into the thorns. They pulled at his clothing and caught in his hair. He hissed in pain, going slowly. The thorns went on forever.

Finnbhear wished he could shift shapes, like his mother. When the mood suited her, she turned into a tabby cat. Finnbhear was sure when he learned to tap his magic, he would be something grander: Like a bear. Then he could push through these thorns with nary a care for his hide.

He emerged, finally, into a small clearing. The thorns circled it, a difficult barrier. Kegal sat in the center, holding his flute. Finnbhear sat in front of him.

"What happens now?" he asked when Kegal did nothing.

"You have to make a sacrifice," Kegal whispered.

Finnbhear examined his surroundings. "A rabbit?" he asked, thinking he could make a snare.

"No," Kegal laughed. "Not that kind of sacrifice. A sacrifice of yourself." He covered his mouth with his hands, stifling his mirth.

Finnbhear took inventory of his person. All he had was his knife and clothes. Neither seemed suitable to give the Sidhe. His grandmother always used to tell him wights like Kegal had no care for either things. They, according to her, preferred things like fresh milk.

Boldly, Kegal reached out and snatched Finnbhear's knife from its sheath. Finnbhear yelled, "Give that back!" and grabbed for it.

"You're likely to cut yourself," Kegal taunted, waving the blade dangerously.

"Give it back," Finnbhear said fiercely.

"We need it for the sacrifice," Kegal reasoned.

"But you said—"

"Your hair," Kegal continued as if Finnbhear had never interrupted. "You have to cut off your hair."

Finnbhear's mouth flew open, his eyes grew round. He tentatively touched his hair, as if it were gone already. "Are you crazy?" he demanded. "My mother would kill me—"

"What does it matter, if you're going to be with me?" Kegal asked. "You want to be my brother, don't you?"

Gingerly, Finnbhear took his knife back. When his first golden lock fell to the earth, he felt a thrill of danger. His mother would thrash him if she knew. If she knew! But he was going to be a wild fairy and do what he wanted. He would never die, would never grow old. And he could grow his hair back.

Kegal rolled on the ground, clutching his sides in mirth. Finnbhear patted his stubbly head, looking mournfully at his scattered hair on the ground. He hoped this was all to the test, and if there were more it would not get worse.

"Now," Kegal snickered, "come on."

They pushed their way out of the thicket. Although the thorns no longer caught Finnbhear's hair, they scratched his scalp. The wounds burned fiercely. Finnbhear gritted his teeth, determined not to cry.

Their next stop was a small cave in the forest. The boys usually pretended it was a troll's hole, filled with stolen treasure and victim's remains. One evening, Finnbhear had went inside and found some bones. They were not two-legged bones but of some other beast. He had taken a skull to show his father and received a sound beating for straying so far from home.

"You know I'm not allowed to be here," Finnbhear almost whimpered. "Father said I could get hurt."

"What does it matter, when you'll be with me?" Kegal said. "Besides, your father isn't around anymore. If you'll recall."

A cruel reminder, but it was effective. Finnbhear bit his lip for silence.

"Go in there," Kegal said, pointing dramatically to the cave, "and steal the troll's tail."

"There is no troll," Finnbhear protested. "Nothing but old bones and dust."

"He was a-hunting last time you came," Kegal said wisely. "But right now he's sleeping. Listen. You can hear his snores."

Finnbhear listened intently, but could hear nothing. He gave his friend a skeptic's glance.

"Just go," Kegal said. "Unless you're a cowering' babe."

Finnbhear considered. A neighbor had caught a troll once. It had been no larger than a dog. Local children used to feed it scraps every evening. There was nothing fearsome about it.

Finnbhear puffed his chest bravely and began to climb the rocks. He slipped once, almost twisting an ankle. His father's warning rang in his ears. Then he thought of returning home, having failed Kegal's test, and continued to climb.

The mouth of the cave was a wide gash facing the sky.

Finnbhear slipped over the edge and lowered himself to the floor. It took a moment for his eyes to filter past the darkness.

There really was a troll, to his amazement and fright. It was a big, furry beast, tucked in a corner like a sleeping bird. His sides rose and fell in slumber. His tail, a ratty thing broken in two places, twitched nervously in the dirt.

Steal that? Finnbhear would sooner get away with flying a large dragon. Almost, he turned to run. Kegal's silhouette darkened the scant sunlight.

"Go on," he hissed. "To be one of us, ye need the guts to do anything! What's the fun of being Sidhe if ye can't enjoy it?"

For the first time, Finnbhear thought about what his friend was. When no one was about, Kegal liked to sneak into the barn and tease the cows. He boasted often about doing much worse in the human realm, such as curdling fresh milk or dumping the cream. Fortunately, most Sidhe respected elves enough to leave them alone.

Finnbhear decided he would be different. He would help people, even humans.

"Hurry!" Kegal hissed. "He'll wake!"

Creeping forward, Finnbhear reluctantly unsheathed his knife and wondered if it was sharp enough. The tail twitched before him like a cat's. It reminded Finnbhear of his mother.

"What if it wakes before I can get the tail?" Finnbhear asked in a whisper.

"You run, dolt!" Kegal snapped.

There was nothing but for it. Quick as he could, Finnbhear pounced on the tail and started sawing with all his might. The tail jerked in his hand as the troll sat bellowing. One last cut and the tail came free, splattering blood everywhere. Finnbhear scrambled back. A gnarled paw swiped at him, barely missing.

"Quick!" Kegal called from the opening.

Finnbhear needed no encouragement. He leaped to the cave mouth to climb out. The troll grabbed one leg and pulled. Finnbhear felt his grip slipping.

Kegal grabbed Finnbhear's arms and pulled with amazing strength. Finnbhear could feel his joints pop, beginning to give way. He screamed.

"My tail!" the troll roared, hauling down.

"My friend!" Kegal cried, hauling up.

"Give me back my tail!" the troll roared again, hauling harder. Finnbhear screamed again, kicking his legs wildly.

"Give me back my friend!" Kegal cried again, heaving another pull of his own.

The troll's grip, under strain from Finnbhear's struggles, slipped. Finnbhear shot out of the hole, crashing into Kegal. Both boys rolled down the rocks, stopping only when a small boulder got in the way. The troll roared from his cave, shaking the ground in his fury.

Coughing, Finnbhear fought to clear the dirt from his eyes. Kegal sat, unhurt, and gave Finnbhear a predatory glance.

"Let me see it!" Kegal asked in delight.

"But the troll," Finnbhear pointed with a shaky hand. No troll had appeared to chase them, but given time—

"He cannae come out in this sunlight," Kegal said. "We're safe, and he'll never catch us once you're a full-fledged Sidhe. Let me see the tail!"

The ground rumbled again. Finnbhear almost dropped the tail. Kegal snatched it, crowing in delight, and danced in circles. The tail looped in the air with Kegal's merriment.

"Let's get out of here," Finnbhear said. The troll still roared below from fury and pain.

Kegal tied the tail around his middle before leading the way. The ends dangled to his knees, yet blended with the rest of his ragtag assortment of dress. Finnbhear would have liked to keep it after what he went through, but he knew from experience not to argue when Kegal lay claim to something. The wight would never let go and disappear rather than fight.

And Finnbhear really did want to become a Sidhe like his friend.

When the troll's fury was far in the distance, they came

upon a small pool nestled in some ferns. Kegal sat on the bank, splashing his feet in the water happily. Finnbhear crouched nearby.

"What now?" he asked when the brown lad said nothing.

"Oh," Kegal said, as if remembering something he had forgotten. "Let me think."

"You're making this up as you go along!"

"Am not," the wight denied haughtily. "But 'tis been long since I took the test, and I don't quite remember all." He placed a thoughtful finger to his chin and tilted his face to the sky.

Finnbhear groaned and settled into a more comfortable position. Just as he started to relax, Kegal leapt up with a shout.

"What a fool I am!" Kegal said, grabbing Finnbhear's arm to pull him to his feet. "All we have left t'do is see the Brown Man!"

"The Brown Man?" Finnbhear repeated in a daze. His muscles complained bitterly as he stood.

"Hurry!" Kegal bade, bounding into the brush like a frightened hare. Wearily, Finnbhear made to follow. It was not long before he was left behind.

What was he to do now? He thought about going home. His mother would have supper cooking. The animals needed feeding. As eldest son, Finnbhear was responsible for the homestead. His little sister was too young to do anything properly.

Then he thought about being a fairy and the delight in store. Kegal always seemed to have so much fun, and he never had to worry about chores. Besides, if Finnbhear was any good at counting, he only had one more trial to go: Sacred practices usually numbered in threes.

Finnbhear forged ahead, vainly looking for Kegal's footprints. The sun was setting fast. With the dark, Finnbhear knew the troll would come hunting for his tail. Fear clutched Finnbhear's breast.

"Hai!" Kegal shouted, jumping from a lower tree limb. Finnbhear stopped dead in his tracks, frozen with terror. The wight laughed.

"'Tis not funny," Finnbhear said.

"Oh, but 'tis." Kegal barked one last laugh before adopting a serious mien. "Are you ready to meet the Brown Man?"

"What for?" Finnbhear asked irritably.

"You'll see," Kegal said sagely. He beckoned, stepping into a copse of trees. Finnbhear followed, not knowing what else to do.

An old man waited for them at the center. He barely reached Finnbhear's height with just the same girth. Dressed in a similar assortment as Kegal, he might have been the lad's grandfather. He blinked with bleary eyes, focusing sharply.

"What have ye brought me?" he asked, scratching his bare chin. Finnbhear stared. He had never seen a shaven man before. It looked odd.

"A new brother," Kegal said stoutly. "See, he got the troll's tail." He flipped one end of the tail.

The Brown Man turned his attention to Finnbhear. He also wore a troll's tail, which he twisted in his knotty hands. "What's this?" he asked. "Kegal, ye idiot, ye've brought me a tree child!"

"Not so," Kegal said. At the Brown Man's disbelieving stare, "Well, mayhaps. But 'tis far in his past. He's mostly elf, now. And he dearly wants to be one of us."

The Brown Man turned his nutmeg eyes back to Finnbhear. "Ye'll be obliged to live in the trees."

"I will," Finnbhear said devoutly.

"Tease the mortals mercilessly."

"Sounds like fun." Finnbhear shrugged. Kegal giggled, his eyes anticipatory gleams.

"Protect the small animals."

"Happily."

"Forsake your mother, your siblings, your father's name."

Finnbhear hesitated. Kegal said, "Ye knew that from the start. I didn't hide it."

"I know." Finnbhear shuffled his feet, feeling very

small.

"If ye want to be one of us," the Brown Man said, "ye must take your knife to your palm. Three drops of blood in Kegal's veins, swearing ye'll be brothers forever. Only by these conditions can ye come to me."

Finnbhear unsheathed his knife, looking at the glint along its sharp edge. It was stained from cutting the troll's tail. Suddenly he felt guilty.

"I thank you," Finnbhear said, sheathing his knife and giving the Brown Man a small bow. "But I don't belong here."

"But, Finnbhear," Kegal protested. It was to no avail. Finnbhear turned and walked from the copse without looking back. Behind him, he heard a satisfied grunt from the Brown Man. Kegal trailed after him, pleading.

By the time they reached the small pool, dark was almost complete. Kegal kicked fallen cones and leaves in dejection. He had not said a word to Finnbhear since the copse.

"I'm sorry," Finnbhear said. "But my family needs me. Without my father, I'm the only man they've got."

"What, so you're talking about growing up now?" Kegal demanded. His eyes bulged, visible even in the dark.

"I suppose I am," Finnbhear admitted, feeling new guilt.

The boys sat for a long moment in the dark, feeling the coolness of the water on their feet. Finally, Kegal stood.

"Been a fine adventure," he said with finality. Finnbhear looked up, trying to see his friend's face. It was rare to find Kegal in a somber mood.

"We'll have more," Finnbhear promised. "Tomorrow. Or in three days at least."

"Oh, aye." Kegal rustled through his rags, pulling something out. He leaned down and placed it in Finnbhear's lap.

"What's this?" Finnbhear asked, touching it.

"A gift for my best friend yet," Kegal said.

With the Sidhe, all things required a balance. Finnbhear's grandmother had often told him that before she died. He offered up his knife and sheath. "Here," he said.

Kegal accepted the gift with a chuckle. He brandished the knife in the dark, making feints at invisible foes.

"Kegal," Finnbhear said, trying to calm his friend, "I need to get home. My mother will be worried."

"No hurry, no hurry," Kegal said. But he took Finnbhear's hand in a friendly grip and lead him through the darkness. Finnbhear trusted his friend, even when he was lead into holes or tripped over roots. It was a rough trip.

"I'm sorry we couldn't be brothers," Finnbhear said when they finally made it. A tallow lamp burned in the window, a sure sign his mother waited up.

"So am I," Kegal said, the closest he could come to an apology. Without ceremony, he turned and vanished into the woods. Finnbhear staggered beyond the trees, too tired to examine his friend's strange behavior.

He stopped once to rub his eyes wearily and touch the stubble on his head. Kegal's gift scratched his eyebrow. Finnbhear examined it, marveled at its coolness. In the dim moonlight he could barely make out what it was. He looked a long time in awe.

The silver flute.

It was too late to call his friend back, to demand an explanation. Something crashed in the distance, a sound like thunder. A wounded troll was looking for a mischievous boy.

Finnbhear faced the welcome light in the window. A small cat leaped onto the ledge, silhouetted against the glow. Green-gold eyes glinted in the dark, pinpoints of fae magic. His mother was waiting.

Her entire world was waiting.

Finnbhear pocketed the flute and went home.

THE SCENT OF WILD HEATHER

This story was written as a companion to my project, Trait of Honor. *Someday I'll have it finished so you can read it. At first, I thought perhaps Lee-i would be a part of* Trait of Honor *itself, but alas. The character was content to settle down and live a boring life after the ordeal I had put him through.*

Well. Nuts to him.

Groggily, Lee-i stumbled out the way station front door and stretched. It was a beautiful morning; the birds were singing, the sun was shining, and in the distance a dragon was doing loops in the blue sky. Yes, it was the kind of day fairy tales were made of. Or, it would have been if he did not have such a damnable headache. Too much wine last night, he reprimanded himself.

How else was he to face those final hours before dawn? On any other day, he could handle the stress of lost urbanites in the jungle or angry elk collisions at the lake's edge. Any other day, rescuing poachers from angry dragon mothers was everyday business. But, today was another story.

He had the day off. It was a special day, the kind of day most thought of as the happiest of a person's life. Today he was to wed the beautiful Arlena of Hutchess Farm.

Arlena, unfortunately, had made other plans.

Damnable women. At the first hint of a bard's song, they run off with every lanky musician they meet. Lee-i scuffed the ground unhappily.

There was a soft step to his right, barely audible. Lee-i's sharp eyes caught the hint of movement in the trees. It sounded human, whatever it was, and clumsy.

Lee-i frowned. Just when things could not possibly get worse, he was going to have to deal with poachers...this close to the ranger station and on the one day he could not hope to control his temper. Even the other rangers had tip-toed around him before they left for patrol that morning; their companion was surly in his pain, difficult to live with.

There was more movement, farther away. Whomever they were, they sounded inexperienced, that much Lee-i could tell. No doubt they were wandering aimlessly, like so many folks did in the woods. It was amazing how many people got lost in the forest every year. Most of them were city folk who had taken the notion that a rough life living off nuts and berries was not only romantic, but easy. Those that survived usually found themselves footing it to the way station via one of the many paths that traversed the countryside.

Lee-i wanted to just ignore the situation and return to his self-pity, but he could not. Even if he was off duty, he was alone. All of the other rangers had gone into the field.

With a silent grumble, Lee-i padded after the intruder and followed them for several kilometers. It was not diffi-cult. Although the intruder's step was light, and he tried to cover his tracks, he was also incredibly clumsy. Broken twigs and trampled grass marked a clear trail for Lee-i to follow.

Despite the temptation to capture this stranger quickly, perhaps with a small leap from a nearby tree to frighten him, Lee-i kept himself a small distance behind and only followed. The ranger was certain that this person was not a poacher, unless he was stupid and starving. Poachers had better sense to stumble along blindly, much less that close to a ranger station with Lee-i standing outside in his most surly mood. The penalty for hunting in the forest, for any reason, was castration or death. Lee-i could have caught the poacher, if indeed he were a poacher and not a romantic idiot, quickly and by surprise. He made the chase a game instead, trying to guess the height and weight of his prey by the size of the occasional footstep or the stray hair. The mental image Lee-i soon had was of a young boy, perhaps about fifteen, with black hair. A city boy, judging by his inexperience with the vast forest.

The trail ended suddenly, as if the intruder had grown wings and flown away. Lee-i stopped, confused, and cast about desperately for more clues. There was nothing. Another man would have been alarmed, would have conceded defeat or searched aimlessly farther on. Lee-i was under no obligation to pursue the chase any further; the idiot would be found one way or the other if trouble came of their presence. But this had suddenly become a challenge, and Lee-i was no ordinary man.

His great distant grandfather had been an ELF, a bioengineered Legionnaire for the Field. "Super soldiers," the old people called them, usually with distaste. Their senses had been genetically enhanced by scientists for war, making them one step above being human. And one step they had chosen to stay, even against excommunication from society. Most people did not trust them, viewed unnatural as they were, and the rest were not comfortable around them.

The ELFs, as they were more commonly called, were all gone now. When the last wars ended, the ELFs were dispersed to civilian lives and the program was shut down. Those that could, lead normal lives by changing their identities. In Lee-i's case, his grandsire had even managed to marry and have children. Most of the ELFs, however, were shunned as they traveled from town to town. The last band of ELFs disappeared into the forest ages ago, and now everyone thought them gone forever.

ELF blood ran through Lee-i's veins, and he knew he was a product of good fortune. Only the other rangers knew about it, even though ELF families were more accepted in his day. In fact, he was a treasured part of the ranger crew, because he reaped all the benefits of his lineage. His senses were extra sharp, his strength twice stronger than the average man's, and his intelligence rated fifty percent higher than average. More importantly, Lee-i was pathic; he could communicate emotion and thought on a psychic level. This was not considered unusual for humans, so much as the intensity Lee-i managed to convey his messages. Even old Jack, who had been a ranger for thirty years, conceded to Lee-i's prowess on occasion.

Admittedly, Lee-i was a little vain about his abilities. Not every descendent carried the genetic DNA, or even the desires, that had made the ELFs special. Those that did rarely had any gift beyond a slight premonition once in a while. But even with just that, Lee-i knew he could capture this interloper and end this game at any time.

He closed his eyes and listened. Quietly, the forest enveloped him, trying to trick his senses. The birds were silent, too silent. The intruder was nearby, close enough to frighten the local wildlife into hiding.

The trees rustled to one another, speaking in their slow,

empathic way. Rain was coming, and they were relieved because the forest had been experiencing a slight drought for the past several weeks. Not once did they mention a stranger in the woods, although a young sapling did wonder idly what the strange man was doing so close to its root system. The stranger had done nothing to harm anything, then. Not that Lee-i was surprised.

The scent of heather drifted down, filled his nostrils, and reminded him of home. No heather grew in the forests of Bellear, where Lee-i was stationed, and only grew wild in the hills of Neissan. Lee-i's thoughts drifted there, land of his childhood, as images of those hills colored purple by that tiny, fragrant flower filled his mind. Suddenly, he was homesick.

His mind was wandering. With a lurch, he forced himself back to the present. His senses followed the scent upward, above the ground, floating on the vibration of recent passing.

Lee-i looked up. Bark fell into his eyes. He blinked it away, grinning. "Okay," he called. "You can come down now."

There was soft cursing in the branches. Slowly, clumsily, a teenage boy made his way to the ground. Nearly slipping halfway down, he recovered himself enough to drop the last few feet, landing catlike before Lee-i. Long hair ruffled in a sudden breeze and was tossed self-consciously.

Glittering blue eyes regarded him with distrust.

Not a boy, Lee-i saw with a jolt. No dark-haired child was this, although Lee-i could have sworn otherwise by the strands of hair he had found. It was a girl, barely in full flower, and half-starved. She wore what once was a pink satin gown; only the bodice remained intact. She wrinkled a freckled nose at him and shook her brown hair from her eyes. The scent of heather clung to her like perfume.

"I don't suppose," the girl said with a strange accent, "that you have anything to eat? I could at least have that before you hand me over to whatever authorities there are in this barbarous place."

Although he was wrong on most counts, Lee-i was right about one thing: This girl was definitely city-bred.

"Come with me," he said, trying to look stern and only managing to sound gruff. He had never been so wrong about anything before, and it disappointed him. "And don't try to run away. I can find you." He gestured toward the way station and began to walk, not caring if she followed or not.

"I guessed that," the girl said dryly. She fell in step behind him and followed willingly. Surprised, Lee-i glanced at her. He had expected more of a fight from this feisty spirit, but held his peace. If he was lucky, she would stay this cooperative all the way to the station.

Once there, Lee-i fed her cold gruel, leftovers from

breakfast. The girl devoured all of it, licked her bowl clean, and then had seconds. Four bowls and six glasses of milk somehow found their way into her slight frame. Lee-i was hard put not to peek into her ears for leakage.

After she was done, she sat at the table with her hands carefully folded in front of her. Was she waiting for an interrogation? It seemed only natural, but Lee-i felt disinclined to bother her. He sat opposite from her and sharpened his knife as if strange girls in the way station were commonplace.

"Well?" the girl finally demanded. Lee-i looked up, coming back from thoughts distant and far away, and again met those blue eyes.

"Well what?" he asked with amusement. "Are you still hungry, then?"

She sighed impatiently. "What are you going to do with me now?" she demanded. "Hang me, give me away, quarter me? Maybe you'll sell me." This last part she said flatly, as if she had been through it before.

He laid his knife aside, slowly so as not to startle her. "I suppose," he said, "you could tell me where you're from. What brings you here, days into the deepest part of the forest? If its romance you've been seeking, I dare say you'll not find it dying from starvation, all alone."

She did not want to answer. It was evident in the toss of her brown mane, the glint in her eye. "I come from overseas," she said. "And I'm here, in this horrid place, because it seemed like a good idea at the time."

Not very straight answers. Or perhaps, they were straight enough not to give anything away. Obviously it was all he hoped to get from her, not that he felt like pressing the subject. "All right," he said, allowing her to keep her privacy. "So what do I do with you now?"

She shrugged. "Do I have a choice in the matter?"

"I suppose," Lee-i said. "So long as I'm convinced you're up to no harm. Most times, when we find someone, we take 'em home. I get the feeling we can't do that for you. So help me out here. Why are you out here, with no provisions...dressed like that? Most people seeking their death come better prepared."

She did not answer. Just when the silence became impenetrable, Lee-i said, "Well, first thing we do, I suppose, is to get you bathed. And dressed into something more than rags." He pointed to the back of the building. "Get going. The tub awaits."

Dubiously, she eyed him to be sure he was serious. He was. She went to the bathtub where it stood in a closet barely big enough for it. Satisfied, Lee-i cleared the table and turned on the sink faucet. Hot water gushed forward, warming his hands, and slowly filled the sink. In tumbled the dishes, and plenty of soap.

Meanwhile, the girl stood at the entrance to the station's

tiny bathroom and stared. Lee-i did not notice at first because he was busy washing dishes. When she finally grew brave enough to step forward and begin looking the tub over, as if she had never seen one before, Lee-i happened to look up. She turned a knob and jumped when water poured out of the spigot.

Overseas, she had said. It made sense. People from across the water were largely ignorant, a technologically impaired, superstitious lot who regarded people like Lee-i as "Demon Folk." So much knowledge had been lost through the years after the wars, and governments like the one Lee-i worked for did nothing to help those poor people over the waters.

He would have to be careful with her, he decided as he dried his hands quickly on a handy towel. Clumsily, the girl shut the bathroom's sliding door. At least he would not be forced to help her there. At least, he hoped so. He threw some old clothes, an old pair of jeans and shirt, over the door quickly, shouting for her to use them. There was no sound within except for running water. Lee-i decided that if she did not come out by dawn, then he would worry.

Much later, the girl emerged from the bathroom. She wore the clothes Lee-i had given her. They fit a little loosely, but it was a definite improvement from her earlier attire. Her hair was wet and sparkled like copper. The scent of heather was dampened and mingled with soap.

"Now that you feel better," Lee-i said, "I need to know. Where are you going? What are you going to do? I'll help you all I can, as will my fellows when they come in from the field. That's part of what we're here to do."

What might have been hope in her eyes died. She slumped back into her chair and stared at her lap. "I don't know what to do," she said softly.

He had found her in the middle of nowhere, half starved to death, wearing rags that once had been fit for a princess, and she did not know where she was going or what to do. Typically female.

"You can't stay here," Lee-i pointed out. "Putting up strangers is strictly against the rules." At the hopelessness on her face, "You can come with me to find our dinner, and after that tell me where you want to go, and I'll do what I can to help you. I promise. You won't be turned away to the cold. We can figure out something. There's the Widow Brown in town; she sometimes puts up folks like you. She's very nice, and I'm sure she'd love you. Meantime, I've got to check the traps."

No response. Lee-i shrugged, picked up his bow and quiver, and walked outside. The scent of heather went with him. He knew the girl was a mere foot behind. He ignored her and concentrated on the snares.

Each was laid in a widening pattern around the station, ready to catch any unsuspecting game that stumbled through. Lee-i was a good ranger, but a lazy hunter. And, with snares, he did not have to be there when his prey died. Sometimes being empathic was a disadvantage, especially when you were feeling that animal breathe its last before your very eyes.

"What is that?" the girl asked when they reached the first snare. A rabbit dangled lifelessly from it, but she did not shy away like most women would have.

"You've never seen a snare before?" Lee-i asked. He cut the rabbit down, looked at the sun, and wished the other snares could wait until evening. "Pity. If you had, you might not have been starving to death when I found you."

She thrust her chin up. "Just because I can't survive in your world," she said haughtily, "don't think you can survive in mine."

Lee-i laughed. The girl deflated visibly. "Wherever did you get the idea I would want to survive in your world?" he said through his laughter. "Lady, you have queer ideas of what other people must think!"

Her eyelashes lowered. Two tears slid down her cheeks, but she made no sound. Instantly, Lee-i felt regret. "Hey, miss," he said. "I'm sorry."

"No," the girl said, biting her lip. "You're right. Teach me, please?"

"Teach you? Teach you what?"

"How to make the snares. How to survive."

It was against his better judgment, but they spent the rest of that day making snares and checking the ones already laid. She was a fast learner. When he told her to skin a rabbit, she dispatched it without flinching. And she was good, like she had done it before.

When he asked her about it, she only shook her head and said, "Not rabbits." Something in her eyes spoke of darkness, and dread. He did not pursue his question, although he wanted to. Something in her eyes would not allow it, and perhaps it was better that way.

The sun sailed westward, sinking below the trees and into the horizon. Lee-i and the girl never noticed. They were inside the way station when it did. The lights there burned bright as noon, the girl had said in awe. Charmed by her ignorance, Lee-i showed her the toaster, the knife sharpener and the oven. She burned her hand, winced, and ignored it. A real trooper.

Privately, Lee-i compared his new charge with Arlena. Arlena, also being from a foreign land, had not known of these things either. When Lee-i had tried to educate his bride-to-be, she politely listened and then returned to her old, more rudimentary way of doing things. Arlena had white-gold hair that fell in soft waves around her apple-smooth face, and eyes of the brightest green. But, all that faded like mist when compared to this new girl's childlike curiosity.

Lee-i and his guest soon shared stew together at the table. Once she felt it was safe, she peppered him with various questions concerning hunting and curing the meat. Trying to answer him as best he could, Lee-i often found himself up against a silent wall full of intimate knowledge, especially when answering questions concerning where and where not to cut an animal's hide. It was disturbing, but Lee-i kept his composure. Surely, the girl would tell him when she was ready, provided she stayed long enough.

The door opened abruptly, and the girl jumped. Jorg and Rose entered, both of them tired and hungry, and paused to eye her. She returned their scrutiny unflinchingly, setting her spoon down as if preparing for further confrontation.

"Well," Rose said, her tousled brown hair shadowing her eyes like fallen leaves, "Lee-i. Who's your friend?"

It dawned on Lee-i that he did not know. He looked at the girl, and she looked at him. Jorg chuckled. "Seems to me," he said to Rose, "that the two aren't sure themselves."

"Her name is Heather," Lee-i said with sudden inspiration. The girl smiled mysteriously into her stew. "Found her this morning, lost in the woods."

Rose thumped down at the table while Jorg ladled out bowls of stew for them both. "Whatever was ya doing out here, girl?" she asked. "You could have died. We can't find everyone that thinks they can make it out here, you know."

"Where are the others?" Lee-i asked, desperate to keep

the topic from delving too far into the girl's situation.

"They'll be staying out overnight," Jorg said, slurping a spoonful of stew loudly. "There was bit of a trouble down by the river. A dragonet. Its mother is dead, mauled by something bigger than it. Earth and sky only know what we'll do about it."

The only thing big enough to maul a dragon was another, bigger dragon. Lee-i whistled appreciatively. It would take all of them to keep that dragonet calm, if they managed to get that far. Left to its own devices, a grieving dragonet could flame the forest down. Rose and Jorg had probably come back to the station to retrieve Lee-i; he was the best of them when it came to mind speaking the wildlife.

Most rangers in Bellear had ELF backgrounds. The inherited gifts from their forefathers and -mothers were what made successful rangers. Few average people survived long in the woods of Bellear, even if they felt inclined to.

Besides dragons, there were mudsnakes, who liked to lay wait along river beds and in streams, predatory cats and dozens of other dangers. If one did not run afoul of these, there were also hidden traps like quicksand or pitfalls. The rangers had a saying about protecting this dangerous environment: Either you were successful, or you were dead.

Those blue eyes were watching him as the girl waited to see what he was going to say. Threats of bereaved dragonets dissolved in the mist of her shining eyes.

"In the morning I'll be taking Heather to the nearest town," Lee-i said. He took a mouthful of stew and chewed on a piece of meat before continuing. "I shouldn't be gone more than two days. Maybe three, if I have to stay overnight. With all of you guys handling that dragonet, you won't be needing me."

Rose and Jorg exchanged a glance. "It's about time you got over that Arlene woman," Rose said finally. "Even if at an inconvenient time."

"Fortunately for us," Jorg said, "the river is on the way to the nearest town. The girl can stay out of the way. We'll set one of the younger ones to protect her, if you're that worried about her safety. But the dragonet is a real threat, Lee-i, and we need you."

Lee-i wanted to protest, but he merely tightened his jaw and pretended to enjoy his meal. Rose, an empath, sensed it and said, "There's no rush to get there tonight. We have the dragonet drugged for now, but in the morning we hope to let it loose. It can't stay drugged up forever."

"But it's pretty upset," Jorg said. "We need you, Lee-i."

It was settled. The four of them struck out into the woods the next day just as dawn was a grey hint in the sky. The girl did not complain as they hiked briskly through the trees, although her breath soon came ragged and her side began to ache. Struggling to keep pace with her companions, she stumbled many times from exhaustion. Out of sympathy, Lee-i demanded a halt. The other rangers sighed, but agreed.

The girl sank to the ground without a sound. Rose and Jorg gave each other a knowing smirk colored with frustration. They were very close to their destination, but the couple remained silent when faced with Lee-i's glare. Lee-i offered the girl some jerky, which she accepted and chewed slowly.

A roar echoed in the distance. Instantly alert, the girl snapped her head up and made a worried, mewing sound. Rose swore. Jorg hurriedly picked up their things, mumbling worriedly. Lee-i helped the girl to her feet.

"The dragonet," Rose said briskly. "They must have lost control of it. Listen. It's headed this way."

Indeed, the crashing of something large thundered around them. That dragonet was moving fast, and when a dragon of any size decided to move the best thing to do was get out of the way. Problem was, however, Lee-i could not decide which way to go. The girl clung to his arm, her breath fast and shallow like a bird's. If she had wings, she would already have flown away, Lee-i thought to himself.

The rangers sprinted toward the sound as fast as they could go. The girl kept pace with them at first, but dropped back as she tired. Lee-i turned then, caught her wrist, and pulled her forward. "I'm sorry," he cried to her, "but we have no time!"

The trees broke suddenly, giving way to grassland and the river edge. The river glittered in the distance like a band of diamonds. Nearby, seven rangers surrounded an adolescent dragon the size of a small hut. Around them, sleep darts and ropes littered the ground. One of the troop, a lad by name of Friedrich, aimed his crossbow loaded with another sleep dart. He fired, missed, then the dragonet swiped him away with an arm.

It roared, flaming into the sky, and thrashed its tail. Rosa and Jorg hurried to join the others, momentarily forgetting Lee-i and his charge. Lee-i pushed the girl against a large tree.

"Wait here," he said. "It shouldn't charge this way, but if it does get out of the way. Fast. I'll be right back."

The dragonet wailed its distress to any who would hear. Its mother was dead, slain by a rival for territory, and now it was alone. How would it feed? How would it live? Quieting, it groaned, sensing a new mind as Lee-i drew close. Unexpectedly, it suddenly roared right in Lee-i's direction. The ranger could feel the waves of grief rolling from it, like cold rolling from a snowbank.

"Be still!" Lee-i called to it as he ran. Standing just under its head, he thrust out every bit of energy he had. He sought its mind and fought to enter, to resolve the knot of panic within. The dragonet fought back with a loud brawl and swatted Lee-i away.

He landed with a skid and sat up in a daze. Hermal, the youngest of them, was at his side. "Can you try again?" he asked breathlessly. His bangs were seared away, and his clothes were scorched. "We may have to kill it if we can't get it under control."

It was against their ethics to kill anything unnecessarily, least of all anything as endangered as a healthy dragon. Their government employed them to guard the forest and its endangered denizens, not to destroy it. Dragons, aside from being almost extinct, were prized as a source of hormones for medicine.

Besides, if they were forced to kill the dragonet, it would mean a year of investigation by the authorities.

This situation had happened one other time, four years before. Investigators from the capital still made surprise visits, to be sure more dragons were not being poached for sale on the black market.

But the dragonet was threatening to burn the forest in revenge for its slain mother. It would see the rival starve before eating the game of its territory. If something could not be done, the dragonet would have to die.

Shakily Lee-i walked forward, back to the dragonet. It noticed him and was surprised. Had not it killed this one already? It lowered its snout, eyes met eyes, and Lee-i concentrated.

What good would burning the forest down do for the dragonet? It would starve, and never grow up to fight the rival and regain its territory. Lee-i felt calm pour through him. The dragonet admitted the truth. Lee-i relaxed.

Suddenly rage boiled back forth. The dragonet did not care. Its mother was gone! Gone! Now it would kill this puny human before it. It would dine on human flesh and become strong, and then it would flame the forest! Drive out the killer! Revenge!

The dragonet lifted a massive claw to take another swipe. It roared its defiance. Dismayed rangers drew their arrows, aiming for the neck, knowing they would have to make them count. Above it all, a young voice rang through the treetops.

"Stop!" She came from nowhere, with arms outstretched, and stood in front of Lee-i. Stunned, Lee-i stepped back as the scent of wild heather overpowered him. The girl stood defiant, legs spread apart. "Stop!" she shouted with her mouth and mind. Lee-i winced. Her voices were deafening.

Pausing, the dragonet cocked its head slightly and stared. The girl stepped forward. The dragonet lowered its head to her and made a lowing sound. She stepped onto its snout and stroked an eye ridge. Lee-i sensed they were communicating on an upper level, beyond his skill. He felt a twinge of jealousy.

A barely perceptible nod from the girl, and the dragonet lowered her to the ground. The rangers still held their arrows ready, but the great beast ignored them. It turned back toward the river and shuffled away. Soon it was crossing to the other side of that glittering band of water and disappearing into the trees. A sense of relief washed over the rangers as they watched it go.

The girl grinned from ear to ear. "Lucky for you," she said, "it has a set of younger sisters to think about. I explained that burning down the forest would starve them as well. It promised to leave well enough alone, until all were strong enough for it to challenge the other dragon properly."

"You're brilliant!" Lee-i breathed. He took her hands into his own. "Simply brilliant!" With her talent and apparent natural inclination for the forest, the girl could easily be the best ranger to ever live. Indeed, to have ever been born. He did not think to ask how she came across the gifts she just displayed, although somehow he knew he should. All he could think about were those merry, blue eyes that were shining as if she were filled with stars.

"Have you ever thought about becoming a ranger?" Rose asked, echoing his unvoiced question.

"You'd certainly make a pretty one," said Thur. He was the handsome one of them. The village maidens swooned over him endlessly.

The girl smiled at Thur, then sought Lee-i's face. He felt a thrill run through him. "No, I haven't," she said. "Before now."

It was a merry night at the way station. After dinner had been eaten and the mess cleared away, Rose played her guitar while the others danced and sang. The girl giggled childlike, clapped her hands, showed an unusual skill on the floor when Thur asked her to dance. She obviously had been taught how, and gracefully. Lee-i traced her bone structure with his eyes. So very delicate, almost birdlike.

They did not notice the knock on their door until it had become a pounding. Their voices and Rose's guitar fell silent, leaving the air oddly alone, while Jorg answered it. As he stepped outside to speak with their guest, the rangers left inside muttered to themselves. The girl, standing beside Lee-i, panted prettily, "Are there more of you?"

The only ranger not there was Head Ranger Vyolen. He was a week's travel away on business in the city. And he would not have knocked, even if he had returned early. Lee-i mused to himself, running possibilities in his mind. The way station rarely had visitors outside of official capacity.

"Heather," Jorg said as he stepped back inside. He was followed by a grey-eyed man. The man bowed to Lee-i and then the others. "Do you know this man?"

She gasped. All color drained from her face, and she

clutched Lee-i's arm in a painful grip. "Krayg," she whispered.

"Sister," the man said with all the show of a loving brother. He ran up to her, crushed her into a hug, but the girl did not return his affection. "I thought I would never find you! Father is so worried, he sits in his study and thinks of nothing else!"

"How did you find me?" the girl choked. She managed to push Krayg away and refused to look at him. "I was so very careful!"

"Tush," her brother said teasingly. "If I told you that, you wouldn't make the same mistake again. Then what would I do?"

"Well, I'm not going back," the girl boldly declared.

"Must we really go through this again?" The man spoke with a barely noticeable sneer. The other rangers shuffled their feet uncomfortably.

Into the silence, Hermal said, "Heather, I'm sure your father is very worried about you. And you can always come back to visit."

"You'd be welcome," Rose said.

"No!" cried the girl. "I won't be able to come back! I won't go with you," she cried to Krayg. "Never!"

Krayg's sneer became more noticeable. "Do you honestly think you can get away?" he said. "You can run, my dear, but you can't hide."

The girl buried her face into Lee-i's chest, who was still trying to climb over his shock. "Please, don't let him take me!" she wailed. She was shaking. It seemed that her stoutness and earlier bravery were a sham in the face of this man. Lee-i placed protective arms around her.

"Listen," he said, "I don't know what exactly is going on here——"

"No, you don't," the man interrupted him coolly.

"And I don't care," Lee-i finished angrily. "She wants to stay. So you can just tell her father that if he wants to see her so badly, he can come here!"

"No!" the girl cried hastily. Shaking her head wildly, she stepped away from Lee-i. His shirt was stained with her tears, and the air cooled his skin in the absence of her warmth.

Her brother laughed. "Not a good idea. Eh, uh...what did they call you? Heather?" Suddenly, he grabbed the girl's arm and jerked her away from Lee-i. "Now, come along. Father wants to see us now."

"Now, see here," Hermal broke in, the peacemaker, "it's dark outside and dangerous. At least wait until dawn." The other rangers murmured agreement, unwilling to see the girl torn away but helpless against a brother's rightful claim.

"No time," Krayg said as he pulled the unwilling girl toward the door. "Sorry."

"LET ME GO!" the girl cried with her mind and body. Lee-i was not the only one who heard it this time. Most of the rangers clutched their heads in pain and moaned. Stunned, Lee-i slumped to his knees.

He looked up in time to see the girl dash out the door. Through his pain-distorted vision, her hair seemed impossibly long and black, and something fluttered behind her. The door slammed back on its hinges loudly.

Krayg watched her go with the patience of a sated snake. He crossed his arms, looked down on Lee-i, and said, "Are you going to chase her, or shall I?"

"What?" Lee-i said as he staggered to his feet. He did not wait for an answer but followed the girl as quickly as he could. The grey-eyed man only stood and watched him go. It made no sense, but Lee-i did not stop to worry about it. Somewhere in the dark, the girl was getting lost.

The moon had risen but was only half full. Despite that, the girl's trail was easier to follow then before as carelessness created more clues for the ranger to follow. She might as well have taken a pail of white paint and marked her path for him.

He found her several miles deep in the woods. Sitting on an old, hollow log, she had her face buried into her hands and wept loudly. Lee-i approached softly, unnoticed, and cleared his throat. She jumped up, ready to run, and saw who it was.

"Lee-i?" she asked, as if unsure it could really be he. "Did Krayg follow you?"

"It's strange, but no," Lee-i said. "What's going on here? I don't understand. He comes all this way to find you, and when you run he doesn't go after you. What kind of family do you come from?"

She only shook her head. "It doesn't matter," she muttered. The sobbing returned, fresh and pathetic. Lee-i gathered her into his arms and held her there against his shoulder. Clumsily, he patted her back.

He closed his eyes and for an instant felt that he was not holding a brunette maid of eighteen. She was a girl of fifteen with hair black as night. Her trusting spirit fell in place more perfectly with this alien vision than the blue-eyed Heather he was coming to know. It was so real, this new vision, that he pushed the girl back to look at her. Her blue eyes, now drying, regarded him from beneath wisps of brown.

"I'll go," she sniffled. "I've put you and your people in danger. And I don't wanna see you get hurt, too."

"What danger?" Lee-i asked incredulously. "What can your brother do against nineteen rangers armed to the teeth?" Softening, he said, "Who's been hurt? Tell me."

Nevertheless, the girl pushed him away. She walked a few steps without looking back. Lee-i followed her because he could do nothing else. "I'll help you," he offered. "You can't survive out here alone."

She was about to protest. He could feel it by how it vibrated around her and how the scent of heather grew stronger. "Besides," he said very quickly. "I promised to teach you how to survive out here. I can't let you leave without that. I thought you wanted to learn more about hunting."

They slept huddled together in the log for warmth. They still slept when the sun rose, and they were sleeping still when noon came and went. When they finally did open their eyes, it was too late to do much in the way of hunting, so Lee-i spent what time he had showing Heather which plants were edible and which plants were poisonous. Her memory was perfect; she knew them all without reminders. They dined on berries and leaves as they walked. Later, the sun sank on their shelter made from leaves and bark, blessed their snares when it rose.

Days went by. Miraculously, the girl's steps transformed from loud and clumsy to sure and quiet. She still had a lot to learn, but Lee-i did not worry so much now. So adept was she, he was certain he could turn her loose and never would she go hungry except in severe conditions.

But the nights, on the other hand, had begun to worry him a lot. Snuggled in his embrace for warmth, the girl was a live thing with delicate breath and collar bones that caught the moonlight like hungry lamps. She was beautiful, no doubt about it, but that was not Lee-i's fear. No doubt she would return his attentions if he tried, but always when the darkness surrounded them, Lee-i was filled with the strong feeling that it was not Heather he held in his arms. He was hard put to place where the visions kept coming from, and so he refrained from anything more than wrapping his arms around her tiny frame.

Sometimes, she looked at him with those enchanting eyes, as if she knew how he ached to have her. Curled eyelashes sometimes would sweep downward as she closed her eyes and smiled softly. Her expression often said she would not mind, and twice Lee-i even reached down to kiss her tender lips. At first, she had stiffened in his arms, but soon softened and curled closer to her friend and protector. Then, with his eyes closed, the vision of that other girl again filled Lee-i's mind. He could not continue.

The second time, two days later, Lee-i tried again, only to find himself so convinced it was a dark-haired girl he held, that he cracked open his eyes even as his lips moved to her willing neck. The scent of heather was strong. He caught glimpses of black hair. Olive skin.

His enhanced sight could not be fooled by night shadows. Neither could his extra senses be telling him wrong, but Lee-i was only confused by what they were saying. He separated from her and sighed. "Sleep," he bade while stroking her brown hair. If she were disappointed, she said nothing. Presently her breathing deepened, and only then did he dare to sleep, too.

He did not try again, even when the temptation was painfully strong. And the girl never said anything. Perhaps she sensed something was wrong, perhaps she did not. Lee-i decided things were better that way.

The moon was waning when they topped the rise where the forest ended and the plains began. It was a marvelous sight. The girl smiled her appreciation as the wind played with her hair. She bore no resemblance to the man who had claimed to be her brother; not now, not during all the time they had spent together.

No details were forthcoming, and Lee-i suddenly realized. He did not want to know. Whomever had hurt her did not deserve to see her again, that much he was sure. He wished he could go with her on the rest of the journey, but he was bound to his job in the forest. There were heavy penalties for deserters, as well as creative ways to find them. Lee-i was forced to content himself with the knowledge that the girl could feed herself when the time came to go.

It was time.

"Follow the setting sun," Lee-i said heavily, waving a hand in a general direction, "and you'll reach Talonia. There probably will be a good captain in port willing to sail you home, to wherever you came from."

Her eyes were wide. "You are not coming?" she asked in obvious distress.

He shook his head sadly. "I'm in trouble as it is," he said. "If I stay away any longer, I'll probably be discharged when I get back. If I'm lucky. I've seen folks beheaded for less than going AWOL a few days." The thought made him scowl. "Besides, I can't cross the border. Talonia and Bellear have a very tentative peace."

She nodded. Her eyes said that she knew all about tentative peace, about borders, about everything. "Thank you," she said gravely, the words escaping her lips like clouds.

"Just go," he said gruffly. She nodded, made her way down the hill, and was soon out of sight.

He had a few hours until sunset. He should have been making the best of it by traveling at his fastest pace. He spent some of it listening to the trees tell him which way she went. The scent of heather clung to him; he breathed it while he could. He walked slowly, nursing the emptiness he felt inside.

A mind shout shattered his melancholy. Heather! He knew it, as surely as he knew himself. Turning, he ran with everything he had. Saplings slapped his face. Roots tripped him in his haste. Another shout echoed through him, guiding him onward.

The plain greeted him with the swishing of grass. He swam it bravely and set his sights on the distant figure of a girl facing off a familiar-looking man. She saw Lee-i, twisted away, and ran for him. The man jumped on her, grappled her, and finally began dragging her away.

It had been building inside of him forever. As despair of losing her washed through him, Lee-i shouted with a power of his own. It reverberated over everything: the grass, the distant trees, the air. Stunned, Krayg lost his grip on the girl, who slumped unconscious to the ground. Panting, Lee-i finally reached them.

"I won't let you have her," Lee-i gasped. "You mean her nothing but harm. I'll fight you for her!"

Krayg's eyes were hard. They reflected jealousy, anger, futile desire. At their feet, the girl slowly opened her eyes and sat. She looked around and wiped her brow with a shaky hand.

"I could kill you," Krayg said, chuckling a bit.

"But she wouldn't like it," Lee-i retorted. "And I can see that you would make her happy, too. So, let her go. She doesn't want to go home with you." His hand reached to his waist, where his knife lay in its sheath. It would be the first time he used it for bloodshed, but he would for Heather.

"Please," the girl said, standing to sway gently. "Please, Krayg. Let me go."

"Haven't you thought that I can't?" Krayg said to her, his grey eyes looking trapped. "That our father would punish me, too?"

Fear of her father. Was that what she was running from? Lee-i started to reach for the girl, but pulled away. She seemed untouchable.

"I'm never gone long. I always come back. You know that. If not then...then..." Her voice trembled, and she licked her lips. "You know what he would do. I can't stay another minute there!" She turned to Lee-i. "It's terrible what they do to me. To us all! You've skinned a rabbit. Imagine...there was a man...And what for, what did that man do to deserve it? Nothing. I can't stand it anymore. I can't!" And she broke into tears, burying her face into her hands, retreating to that familiar gesture for comfort.

Lee-i touched her arm, unsure of what to say. What kind of people were these? Could he hope to fight against someone like Krayg and win? He would try, for her. Sickened at the thought of what the girl had just said, and the things she never could, Lee-i pulled his knife from its sheath.

"I will fight you for her," Lee-i said again.

Krayg did not answer. His eyes were focused inward, as if he, too, did not want to face the horrors at home. Lee-i thought of his own ancestors, who had been created as instruments of the most wicked deeds of war. He wondered if they could compare to what he was seeing hints of in that moment.

Wiping tears from her eyes, the girl stepped toward Krayg and held out her hand. "You have a token of my faith, hidden away with the old man. Just for a little while, Krayg. Please."

Silence stretched out immeasurable. Krayg finally nodded, too choked to speak. Lee-i could not believe it was that easy for her; to talk her way into freedom from someone so set on keeping her. Then he remembered the dragonet, and somehow it all fell into place.

She smiled and giggled. She threw her arms thankfully around Krayg's neck, who looked shocked but returned the embrace fervently. Then she turned her affection to Lee-i, who nestled her hair and breathed in the smell of that tiny flower. The image of the other girl rose before his eyes. Suddenly, he was holding her.

She winked a bright eye at him and then she was Heather, normal-looking and extraordinary. Lee-i stammered, wanting to ask what she was, how could she be there. Why could she not stay? Would he see her again? He pushed it down.

Were these Demon Folk? he wondered, his eyes flicked from one face to another. Was there a basis to the old tales and superstitions?

The girl was kissing him, passionately. He responded, helplessly caught in his need for her. I hope you have the sense to stay away, he thought to her.

I will, she returned. It startled him, this rare use of talent. She smiled sadly, slipped out of his arms.

Then she was gone, making her way through the grass and toward Talonia. Too soon, she became a silhouette against the setting sun. Something fluttered, and then even her silhouette disappeared. Lee-i blinked, unsure of what he had seen, or even if wings that size were possible.

Krayg had left without a sound. Lee-i did not know the man was gone until he looked around, intent on pressing his questions to him. There was a faint odor which destroyed the cloying perfume of the girl's passing.

Demon Folk. Lee-i speculated that he was going insane, or perhaps this was all a dream. The old women said that Demon Folk were elusive, keeping deep in the forest where even the rangers would not go. They possessed powers of transportation, shape-shifting and telepathy. Just to name a few. But those were all myths, or so Lee-i had always thought.

Old folk also said Demon Folk were descendants of the ELFs.

Some ELFs, so it was said, could not adapt to civilian ways after the clinics that birthed them were closed forever. They had spent their entire lives at war. Peace was quite a culture shock. Their answer to that problem was to make a new home for themselves. No one quite remembered where. Only other ELFs, or children of the ELFs, ever made their way to it. So it was said.

Mingling with human stock had kept Lee-i's family relatively normal. The Demon Folk, pure-blooded as they were, had a problem. Each generation was born more powerful than the last. Strange spawned stranger until their humanity was gone.

Perhaps that was what the scientists had in mind when first they tampered with the ELFs' genetic makeup. No one alive knew. Except the Demon Folk, who might still hold such secrets in their lair. If they existed.

Lee-i blew out noisily and turned back toward the forest. He would never see the girl again, whatever her origin. It would be a lonely trip back.

He was not the same man after that, the other rangers were often heard to say. Rather than explain what had happened on his jaunt through the forest—as Hermal described it—he took six months in solitary as punishment for going AWOL. And he withstood his sentence like a martyr, taking that time to contemplate his lost Heather and the man who chased her. When he was released, he went home.

After a tentative courtship, he married a childhood sweetheart and brought her to Bellear. His wife brought potted plants with her to remind them of home. There were blue gardenias, purple spiders, a young mimosa, foxgloves, lilies, bleeding hearts, and heather.

The heather died within a year. It was the same year

that Lee-i's first child, a daughter, was born. They named her Aisse. Time marked its passing with the turning of leaves. Aisse took her first steps and learned to fire a bow. If anyone asked, she told them she was going to become a ranger like her father. She had the gifts and liked to practice them on her numerous pets.

Lee-i grew content. His nights were never lonely, he was respected by his peers, and never did without. The gods had been kind.

He never forgot the sweet scent of heather. And after a while, he stopped trying.

Strings Below♪
Katrina Joyner

STRINGS BELOW

*"**I used to think** I was the only one who could hear them. Yeah, I thought I was going insane. It's funny, but once you reach the other side you realize that you're not the crazy one."*

She still shyly skirted at the edge of the group, listening intently with expressive eyes. No one quite remembered where she had come from. The higher ranks noticed her only as needed, although they picked her the most because of her speed. Then they would point, or nod, and say, "Small One." Obediently, she would step forward, receive her instructions, and fly away.

Mostly, she carried messages from layer to layer. She spent more time traveling on the universal ties, or the strings, than anything else. Her thoughts raced with her on those journeys, lingering often where she could not visit again.

The last time they picked her, she flew to the edge of the universe. There were very few stars there, and the vast emptiness made her feel large and at peace. Lingering, she felt herself drawn down a spiral string to the warm planet. For a long time, she hovered to watch clouds drift over the ocean. Something within her moved with them, so she pushed away and sped back to her masters. When she arrived in the round space of their meeting hall, she hid in the dark.

She watched as the others were chosen one by one. They sang ceaselessly, their wings catching the sound and pushing against it. As they passed by, their light streaked across the darkness. The small one traced the images with her mind, unconsciously humming to herself. Blackness coated her as she tucked her own wings closer to her body.

The masters were tall people; their songs had made them so. They towered over her like redwood trees. She used to be terrified of them but eventually realized that they had never hurt her.

Now they were very agitated. Even their discussion was dissonant. Some made short gestures with their arms. Methane clouds roiled, flashing with bursts of electric energy. The small one dipped into one and slid forward.

"It doesn't matter how it happened," the tallest of them was saying. "He's gone. That's what is important. We have to figure out what we're going to do."

"Without him?" another snapped. She was no one the small one had ever seen before.

"We'll have to find a replacement," said yet another.

"Do you know how long that will take?"

"Don't we all?" The tallest surveyed his companions. "We can't save him. The idiot went below."

The others were silent, some looking down. The air felt gravid with implication. "He'll lose his breath," someone whispered after a moment.

"There's nothing we can do," the tallest said. "We can't go, and the tendrils couldn't withstand a trip like that."

There's nothing we can do. The statement smacked inside of the small one. Someone had said that once before, long ago. That was when she first came to the layers. Most of the memory was lost to her, but if she tried she could recall the sting of salty water in her nasal cavity.

"We should begin the hunt for his replacement," the tallest said. The others did not look happy. Hesitantly, each one nodded.

"Where shall we begin?" asked the shortest of them.

The small one stepped out of her shadow, but did not speak. No one noticed her, even when she spread her wings and dove. The note she used to push herself forward was shrill. It parted the clouds violently, but they quickly settled back into place.

"Sometimes it feels like my memories multiply all by themselves, and all I want to do is scream. But you can't scream out there. You can only sing, because that's what keeps you alive. I used to love music."

The small one had never been below. She had heard others speak of it, but tendrils like herself were never sent in that direction. Like the masters said, it was a dangerous place. Space was thick there, and the pressure could crush her. Sometimes stars were born there, but most of the elements were grey and unable to support life.

Regardless, she let momentum propel her down until

she reached the end of the universe. The astral membrane which divided the layers resisted her just enough that she had to force her way through. She popped into the other side; the middle layer, where the stars lived.

Another tendril passed diagonally by, the tip of its wings barely missing her nose. She changed direction to follow and soon caught up to it.

"I need directions," she said. The other did not stop slipping forward, although it did turn to look at her.

"You're not like the rest of us," it observed. It beat its wings faster, but the small one matched its pace with a single feather flick. "Go away."

"I need directions," the small one repeated patiently. "Tell me how to get below."

At first, the other one ignored her. It dipped through the strings, using sharp twists to fly faster across the fabric of space. The small one kept abreast by jumping across the cables and using backward thrusts of her wings.

"If you don't tell me," the small one finally said, "I will tell the masters that you refused to help me deliver a message."

The other thrust itself violently ahead so that the string it rode vibrated. A G note warbled into the layers towards the outer edges into eternity.

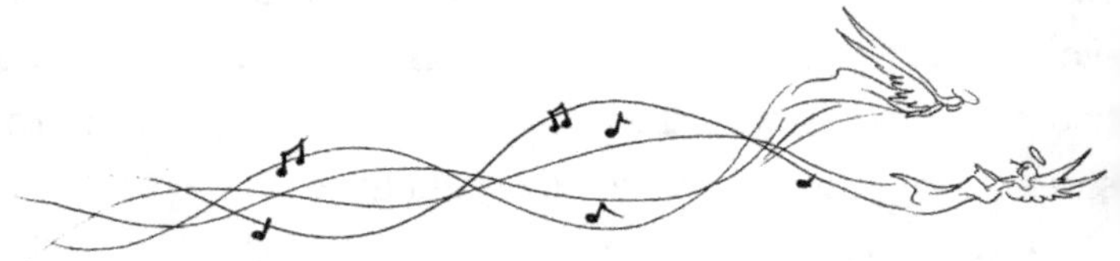

"They don't like us to go there," the other said irritably. "If you go, you won't make it back out again. You lose your breath down there."

"I have to go. Please tell me the way."

The other frowned, beating its wings fiercely for a moment. "They wouldn't send you below. They never send us below."

"But it's like you said. I'm not like the rest of you."

It frowned further, but could not refute her logic. "You go straight," it said. "Go until you reach the bottom. If you go too far, you'll lose your breath. You're stupid for going." It flipped itself out of the string, which vibrated from the disruption. The sound spread out in C waves.

The small one rode one of the downward waves, taking advantage of the force to rest her wings. She passed by small moons, skirted a black hole, but barely noticed these everyday occurrences. Her mind was centered on her goal. If she managed to get below, she could find the master. She had no doubt about that. That was what her kind did. But, going straight was not as easy as it sounded. The strings shifted positions often so that most twisted in confusing ways.

The small one sometimes thought of them as roller coasters.

If she hit an empty space without strings or even dark matter, she would have to use her own energy to fly. This always tired her. What if she got too tired to sing? One of the masters had placed symphony into her so that she could cohabit with them. If that song died, so would she.

Smoke and green clouds rose around her as she rode the note. She avoided them as best she could, not wanting to be sucked into the center by their gravity. Inside, infant stars chimed off key. When they were fully formed, their notes would harmonize with the rest of the universe. Until then, they quavered oblivious.

After a while, the wave faded into silence. After that, the small one glided until she finally had to fly. The stars were farther apart, and the open darkness below was thick. There was not a string in sight. It hardly seemed a place one of the masters would fly.

When she finally reached the membrane between layers, she rested against the smooth surface. Her wings ached. The space around her was oppressive. She sang to herself for a while without moving; it was more for comfort than anything else. Memories of a loving face singing lullabies surfaced in her mind. The small one closed her eyes, basking in it.

> *"You can't let fear hold you back. Yeah, they said there was nothing that could be done. Well, what do they know?"*

She put her hand on the membrane, feeling the energy move beneath it. Hopefully this was all she had to do to get below; push through this membrane into the unknown beyond. Oddly, she felt no fear. She looked up. Stars twinkled at her from far away.

Without any further hesitation, she stretched her wings and pushed against the membrane. It was not as hard as she expected it was going to be. Before she knew it, she was through.

The first thing she noticed was the turbulence around her. The space was filled with knives of sound, which cut her tender flesh. She squealed and tried to jump back up through the membrane and to the space above.

The membrane resisted despite her desperate 

attempts to claw through. She fluttered against it wildly, singing higher the more she was cut. At last, she gave up and wrapped her wings around herself. Shielded, she let the space pull her to its center.

Grey matter sped by. Frightened, she spread her wings and tried to regain control of her flight. Sound no longer cut her flesh, but she could feel the air pressing with a heaviness that grew the farther she fell. Zigzagging around unidentified particles, she tried to spiral her way back towards her heaven.

It was the first time she was not fast enough. The air was just too heavy; her notes could not carry well. The only thing she could do was keep falling, so she did with her eyes closed. After a while, she stopped singing. It was too hard to breath.

"Sometimes I have to listen hard to make out what the voices are trying to say to me. They don't usually say anything bad. You know, they tell me things to make me feel better about something."

She landed on something cold and flat. The force of impact momentarily knocked the rest of her breath out so she lay gasping like a fish. Involuntarily, she thought about the acrid feel of water in her nostrils. "I've been here before," she thought to herself.

With clenched teeth, she got onto her hands and knees. Around her, grey matter stretched out as far as the eye could see. Without a doubt, she was below. She wondered if there was any way to go deeper into the layers. Then, she remembered why she had come.

She had to use her wings for support, but she got to her feet. Now that she was there, she had to find the missing master. There was an unforeseen problem, though. Things were so chaotic; she could not get a sense of where he was. She was already beginning to feel lightheaded from being unable to breathe properly. The sky mocked her from above.

If she were in any of the upper layers, where things made sense, she would only have to trust her feelings. The small one closed her eyes, trying to ignore the burning pain of her entry wounds. She would know where the master was. She just had to trust herself. In the end, she randomly picked a direction. The terrain around her did not change as she dragged along. She kept her eyes on her feet.

The world blurred from time to time. She stumbled, falling face first in a heap. Maybe there was nothing that could be done. She was a fool to help someone who only noticed her when he wanted something. Now she was going to perish alone.

She sang to herself, softly, because it seemed better than crying. The music she made was not the pointed notes she used to fly through the layers. There were words in her song; sad words that cried for her.`

"…who…?"

The voice was faint, almost too faint to hear. She tensed, listening.

"…singing….?"

She recognized that voice! The small one struggled upright while her wings beat wildly. "Master! I'm here. I'm right here."

"…here."

She found him underneath a strange outcropping. It formed a natural shelf and protected him. He had diminished; now he was but a fraction of her size. He barely looked up when she came to him. Grateful for the miracle, she rested and listened to his shallow breathing.

"I've come to get you out of here."

It felt odd to be so close to one of the masters, and yet he did not tower over her.

"What are you doing here? Why did you come?" The master did not respond, nor did she think he heard her. "Wake up. Wake up!" She reached out to shake him, but hesitated. What would happen if she touched one of the masters? No one touched them. They did not even touch each other.

Carefully she leaned down and put her lips very close to his ear. "You have to get up. I'm here to take you home." It was getting harder to talk. Waves of dizziness crested over her. "Please get up." The last sentence was a mere whisper.

The master did not respond, nor did he stir. The light of his song was almost gone. She thought, "How can we keep singing in such a muddy atmosphere, anyway?" This place was all wrong.

"I will carry you," she said more to herself than the being that lay prone before her. "You will be my message to the others."

In her homeland–that place of salty water and loving faces–she had also carried messages. There had been love letters scented with perfume, shopping catalogues, and brief notes dealing strictly with business. She was sure that she had been very good at her job.

In this world where thoughts took form and music carried power, she turned messages into light and tucked them deep within her essence. She was unsure if she could do this to her master, but she had to try. She lay over the master's body, singing her own special note. At first, nothing happened. Suddenly the master stirred and moved. He nestled very quickly into her abdomen. Her world lurched with the action, and she retched on the spot where the master had been.

"There were those that begged me to live, yeah. But then that one guy said there was nothing that could be done, and I felt myself floating away from everything I knew. The voices were calling

me, you know? Sometimes I wish that one guy had wanted me to live, too."

In the sky, grey matter swirled. Things like this never happened in other parts of the astral cosmos, but she knew what was happening. She had seen it before. Acid rain splashed onto her face to leave burning trails where it ran. She could not scream – she just did not have the breath to do so anymore. Her abdomen felt heavy.

The rain thickened and formed puddles at her feet. "Please lend me strength," she prayed to her master before bending her knees for the leap of their lives. She let forth the highest note she could. It fell short in the unreceptive environment. Inside of her, the master shifted his weight. It felt strange, and she grunted a low note.

That was the note that cascaded around her. Its echo stained the air, almost puncturing the surrounding pressure. Without thinking, she cupped it with her wings and thrust herself forward. Like an arrow freshly released, she soared upward. The motion helped her to gain a new breath.

The rain beat against her as if the universe would keep her down, but that only encouraged her to fly faster. With each new gasp of breath she managed to steal, she put out a string of constant low notes. Up and up she went, thinking about a song she used to know. She was climbing for heaven.

"When I first got here, I thought this place was beautiful. But it's pretty like a cotton candy is pretty. There's no substance, you know?"

When she reached the dividing membrane, it took everything she had to sing her lowest note. That was just enough to help her punch through. The membrane vibrated violently. Sound waves exploded outward and pushed her farther away. Gratefully, she let them take her. The weight in her middle acted like an axis, making her pivot in dizzy circles.

After she had stopped spinning, she let herself drift. The master stirred in her womb, feeding on what energy she had left. It was too soon to release him back into the cosmos. He needed to be where he belonged first, and that meant she had to continue to fly. "Master, I'm so tired," she said to no one in particular.

At first, she did not know where she was. To her right loomed one of the star nurseries. The methane clouds flickered with light, like a candle lit in a window. She decided to head for that, and perhaps she could get her bearings from there.

She flew slower than before. The weight of her burden dragged against her like an anchor. To her, it was an eternity before she finally reached the outer fringes of the methane clouds. Little lights danced around them; the others of her kind were there, running their endless errands.

It was very tempting to rest there, but the small one did not. She followed the others, trying not to pause as often as she needed to. Her voice was hoarse, and her wings were numb from overuse. She passed many strings by, knowing that she did not have the strength to use them. She could feel her light dimming.

Just when she thought she could not sing another note, nor pull herself forward on yet another wave, the masters' central hall came into view. "We're almost there," she told herself, touching her belly as if to comfort her cargo.

> *"Sometimes I think these memories aren't real and I'll never find who I really am. Then there are times that I believe with all my heart. I really don't know. But, who really does?"*

Of this moment there are at least two perspectives. In the small one's memory, she entered into the room with a weak croak. The clouds that covered the room's floor filled her eyes, and she had to push herself past them.

She was frightened. She had never directly addressed the assembly before, and she not only touched her master but carried him inside. What were they going to do to her? The weight in her womb shifted again just as the clouds cleared from her eyesight.

The masters, still in deep discussion, did not notice the small creature rise above the clouds with a thrust of her wings. She hovered there, politely, until she realized that she had to catch their attention. "Listen to me. Look! I bear a message," she sang.

At first, those on the outside were the only ones to look. Then, the tall one in the center turned towards her. That was what she needed; it was what all of her kind needed.

… She birthed a god…

The pain was soon forgotten as her hold on consciousness slipped. Her master stepped amongst his brethren reduced, but whole. Her life essence had given him the sustenance he needed. The last sight she had before passing out was their controlled reunion.

> *"One of these days, I'm going back and the voices are going to leave me alone. I'm going to know who I am. I'm going to love music again, and I'm going to dance. I'm going to learn to fight for what I believe in."*

A second perspective comes from the eyes of the assembly. Their discussion had grown heated. Some wanted to replace their missing companion, and others felt that they could continue without him. The tendrils were being worked extra hard as numerous messages were sent to various corners of the universes. At least one master had even created more tendrils to make sure things got done.

That was when Small One rose out of the clouds. She was different somehow; her light was phenomenally bright as if she overflowed with power. She said something before screaming a melody that disrupted the harmony of their council.

A god was born; he emerged from her womb like a newborn infant. Small One shuddered from the pain before collapsing into the clouds. Her surrogate son floated with his own light, but she still outshone them all where she lay half-hidden.

The son took his first steps and reclaimed his place with a simple nod. It was plain that he was not as strong as before, but he could still do his job. That was all that mattered. The dilemma ended, more tendrils were sent to cancel previously sent messages.

Then, the masters all turned on the exhausted Small One.

> *"They won't let me forget, though. I'll always remember."*

Compassion was not something the tall ones were very familiar with, but they knew and understood gratitude. "This one saved my life," her son said. "We should do something for her."

"You don't thank a tendril," said one of the others. "It's unheard of. Tendrils are nothing more than extensions of us."

"She is not a tendril," said someone else. "She came to us a short time ago, and I allowed her to stay. She looked so pathetic, what else could I do? I couldn't just let her die."

The small one's son was the first to kneel by her side. "I say we give her life. It's only fair."

"It's the least we can do," said the next to kneel, the one

who let her stay in the first place. "I second the motion."

"Very well," said the tallest. "Let's get this over with. We have a lot to do, and there is so very little time to do it in."

They surrounded the small one, and then they touched her. Some did so reverently, smoothing the hair from her forehead in loving caresses. Others gripped her arms violently, darkening her light with astral bruises. Some did so sexually, fondling regions that would have made her blush. They touched her placidly, uncaringly, and curiously. There was not a portion of her body left unsacred.

The small one's eyes fluttered open just as the tall ones stepped back. Her son kissed her brow slowly. When he pulled away, a residue of light soaked into her skin. "You are a messenger no more," he said to her. "Stand up, Small One. And please. Stay here a while."

Amazed at how good she felt, the small one got to her feet. Her wings no longer ached, and her song felt stronger than ever. Her son towered over her the way he had always done, but somehow that was different. No longer a mark of rank, it felt more like a mark of individuality. The small one decided that she liked that.

As she looked into each of their eyes, she realized that they wanted her to live.

"Yeah, I hear voices. They sing to me. And when I'm feeling especially depressed, they do their best to cheer me up. That's what friends do. They remind me that somewhere out there, a sun is always rising. I'm going back there, someday. And when I do, I'm going to sing.

I used to love music."

OF MELODIES AND MEMORIES

One of my first publishing achievements, even though I was only in high school and it was in the school magazine, Serendipity–1989. Not everyone got into that magazine, by jove!

Play it again," Rael pleaded. The summer winds played in her long, blond hair. Flower petals littered themselves onto the grass from her delicate plucking.

Sifu lifted his wooden pipe to his lips and played a tune both soft and spirited. The winds carried the notes far over the meadows, then changed themselves with the song. They caressed Rael's soft face and rustled through Sifu's platinum hair. All the while, Sifu's pale, grey eyes gazed into Rael's own black, and they both remembered how they met, the time shared between them and the many words spoken to each other.

The tune ended. The winds calmed. Rael's ears strained to catch the last notes of the elfish melody. The elf admired his love, all ready composing another melody to please her.

"Just one more time," Rael whispered, "and then I must

return home before Mother realizes I am away." She lowered her eyes in a blush. "One day, Sifu, I promise I will return to these woods forever."

"I know," Sifu said before placing the pipe back to his lips. The wind danced and the summer flowers sang as the elfish trees listened with slow patience.

The song ended. Lips embraced briefly. Rael was gone, but only to return on the morrow. Sifu stood alone, remembering her walk, her face, her voice.

They were in love.

SLINGSHOTS

This story is part of the World Akashik, the universe to a couple of my comics. Originally the main protagonist was Taus from the other stories, but I no longer consider this story canon for her and have changed names.

Sipoo idly pushed a few buttons on the console then flipped a switch to release thrusters. Things lurched slightly when she opened backward thrusts, putting the ship into break formation. Blinking lights reflected in her eyes as they scanned the data screens avidly.

Herman studied the preoccupied expression of his partner. She seemed more interested in her thoughts than aligning their little space freighter into a safe orbit. When she got like this, Herman tried to get out of town. It worried him that this time he was already out of town and she had come along for the ride.

"Where in the nebula are they?" Sipoo muttered to herself.

"Maybe we're parking on the wrong side," Herman suggested. Before them, an immense blue-white star roiled angrily in the silence of space. Sipoo was still making orbital adjustments to account for gravitational pull.

"These are the coordinates," she said. "If they chicken out on us, I'll make sure to post it across every bulletin board in the ethernets from here until Sunderland."

"You're so sexy when feeling vengeful," Herman remarked. "Lucky for me, this means you're sexy all of the time."

"Shut up," Sipoo said, hiding a smile. Folding her arms, she contemplated the gaseous monster before them. She was thinking very hard about something. It would be a little while before she felt amicable again, if at all.

Herman stood up and stretched. It had been a long ride since leaving the comfort of that little bar on Station Black Prime. His back hurt from sitting down at the console for so long. "I'm getting a snack. Want anything?"

"Water," she answered. She had turned her attention to the local area scan.

Water. This was not a good sign. "Be right back," Herman said. He was almost to the exit when the ship's console started to bleep. Sipoo barked a quick laugh.

"They're here," she announced unnecessarily.

Resigned, Herman returned to his seat. "Don't hail them yet!" Sipoo cried, slapping his hand away from the frequency dial. "I'll be right back. If they hail us first, fine. You know what the plan is, right?" She escaped the room before he could answer.

Herman knew that Sipoo had a plan. Like usual, he was never clued into the specifics until it was too late. He went along with Sipoo's plans because they usually ended happily with money, liquor, and a night he couldn't remember. Besides, she would kill him if he did not.

This plan's objective was probably no different. However, they were parked by a giant star a trillion miles away from civilization to meet with questionable people. The situation simply screamed, "Arrest me!"

Communications blipped quietly. Herman looked at the area scan. Two ships had slipped into orbit like gentle thieves. That had to be them calling.

Herman turned on the telescreen and patched the call through. "This is *Dying Sun 009*," he said. "Go ahead."

The serious face on the screen had a hard-pressed mouth. His graying hair glinted from the console lights. There were fine wrinkles around his eyes. He wore a dusty fighter jacket, the kind that soldiers wore. His hard green eyes narrowed. "Let's get this straight," he said. "The first one who breaks thrusters loses everything."

"If that's the agreement," Herman stalled. He turned to ultrasound and ran a scan on the ships. One ship drifted closer to the *Sun;* the other held its distance from them, observing the two in a silent cold stare.

"Where is the woman?" the man asked. "Where is my challenger? I'd like to see her for real, instead of talking to her over sound frequencies."

"She's preoccupied," Herman responded, looking down at the scanner's report. The two sleek ships were built for speed and stealth. Blondie's ship was obviously just a speedster; a toy for the rich. From where it held a safe distance, the second ship was much more dangerous. It possessed a dazzling array of weapons- any one of them would fetch a handsome price on the black market. Herman noted that each of the weapons was in firing range of the two ships. "I can have her call you back." Without looking up, he adjusted one of the controls.

"Is she even real? Ha! She left you to run this race by yourself, didn't she?" the man accused. "Look at me when I'm talking to you!"

Abandoning Herman would not be like Sipoo, but he would never admit that to a stranger. He broadened his scan to the surrounding area. "Just tell me the conditions," he said. There were no other ships nearby. This was a very private deal.

The door behind Herman opened abruptly, and a strange woman stepped on deck. She had short, spiked red hair and a realistic tattoo across her face. Sipoo's disguise was so complete, he barely recognized her. She even wore a flight jacket similar to the one their opponent was wearing.

She swaggered to the video screen and leaned against one of the consoles, thrusting her hip out. "Well," she drawled, "so *this* is what you look like."

"Yes. It would appear so," the man said. "You must be Emerald Briggs."

"Former Private Briggs, at your service!" Sipoo saluted tightly. "A pleasure to meet the infamous Corporal Reginald Jones! And an honor to race against you, sir!" She laughed, slamming herself into her chair and propping her booted feet up.

Corporal Jones grunted. "I've never heard of you," he said. "Now that I've scanned your ship, I'm appalled you would have the brass to challenge me."

Herman started to say something, but Sipoo cut him off. "She may not look like much to the untrained eye, but *The Sun* can take it," Sipoo boasted.

"You're piloting an obsolete class freighter," the Corporal snapped. "You don't stand a chance. I will give you this one chance to concede, with no embarrassment for your side."

Sipoo patted the closest console lovingly. Since joining Herman as his partner, she had invested a lot of her personal savings in fixing up the ship. The engine had been rebuilt, corroded fuse lines and circuitry had been replaced, and exterior items had been added.

"These are my conditions," she said. "Fifteen shots around this star. The closest one—"

Herman tried to interrupt. "Excuse me—" Sipoo kicked him underneath the console.

"—wins. The first one to blink loses. If I win, I get your ship or the monetary equivalent. We'll start from sixty thousand specters off starboard."

"When I win," the man said smugly, "I'll be sure to set a memorial beacon for your death."

"Whatever works," Sipoo quipped before hanging up on him. She smiled as she turned to the control console. Herman gaped at her horrified; Sipoo kept her smug smile and ignored him.

"Are you insane?" Herman demanded as Sipoo broke orbit. He was thrown off balance as *The Sun* veered wildly away from the star. "You challenged Corporal Jones to a *slingshot race?* He's one of the most ruthless underground pilots in space! We'll be fried in the sun's photosphere!"

Sipoo shrugged. "Don't be so optimistic. Anyway, didn't you race once upon a time? You've earned a bit of your own reputation through the years."

"I can't beat this man!" Herman shouted. "Especially not using *The Sun!* She's not built for this sort of thing!"

Sipoo did not respond. She was so engrossed in piloting them to the designated starting point, she might not even have heard him. "We're going to die," Herman tried again.

After another minute of silence, he gave up. It was too late to argue the point, anyway. If they backed out of the fight now, the third ship would open fire. It was not with them to race. It was there to make sure there was a race in the first place.

Slingshot racing… It was drag racing while using a star's gravitational pull to fly faster and in tighter orbital circuits. The winners (or survivors) were pilots who managed to skim the closest to the star without being pulled into the fire. Losers pulled away, braked, or simply did not make it out again.

There was a reason why most governments had outlawed the fine art of playing chicken with a star's gravitational pull. Although there was never a mess to clean up because all of the casualties burned to a crisp in the star's photosphere, the death count was staggering. Banning the practice had only made it more popular, though, and it had become the most popular game for high stakes gambling. Could his partner have picked a more dangerous means to make some quick cash?

Sipoo turned on the outward monitor to get a more natural view of their surroundings. Her face flickered with an unreadable emotion as she pondered the star. One fist was clenched against her hip. Gods, Herman realized. She was unconsciously standing at attention.

He knew that she had once served in the military, but it

had never before hit him how much of an ex-soldier she was. Her flight jacket looked well-loved; polished and oiled to keep the leather soft. She even had put an insignia cuff on her ear. It was not a private's cuff, but something for a higher rank. Having never paid attention to such things, Herman was not sure which one it was.

With the outward monitor running, they were able to watch the other two ships break their own orbits to join them. "How much are we paying the other guy to referee?" Herman asked. The Corporal's ship was almost in position next to them. The third ship slowly drifted closer to the port side. One of its main cannons was fixed on the *Sun*.

"The corporal is," Sipoo said with a grin. "I told him that that since he expected to win, he could expect to foot the bill. He's so full of himself, he didn't even argue with me." The corporal's ship was in place. Sipoo punched a call out on the telescreen. Corporal Jones' face immediately filled it.

"We'll go when the ref signals," Sipoo said. "You might want to tell him that."

"Tell her yourself," Jones snarled. The image on the screen split into two as he patched their referee into the conversation. On one side of the screen was the corporal. On the other was a delicate-looking, pale woman. Herman cocked an eyebrow, wondering what she was doing after the race.

She wasted no time. "I will make it clear that I am completely neutral in this affair." Her voice was soft. "If either of you frag off, I will open fire with everything I've got. If either of you fly on computer automation, I will open fire. If either of you break a single rule, I will open fire. Got it? Good. I will signal in ten." The monitor went dark.

Herman swiveled his chair to face Sipoo. "This is stupid. We're slingshotting against a dangerous shot pilot with a ring dust referee. We're going to die."

"We'll be fine. Trust me on this." She had produced a rag from one pocket and was using it to clean her face. Her skin was red from her furious rubbing.

"So, think you can fill me in on what's exactly going on?"

"Get ready, the signal is starting." Sipoo tossed the rag aside and jumped to engine control. "Warming thrusters. Looks like all go in five."

Herman barely had time to cue the computer into manual. The referee ship blinked its outer lights brightly twice, and Sipoo slammed her hand on the button console. *The Sun* jumped forward just after the corporal's ship. As the star got larger in the monitor view, the corporal's ship got smaller as he left them behind.

"Frag it!" Herman cursed.

Sipoo's smirk was mysterious. "Our cargo will speed us up when we need it. That star is our propulsion system, remember? We're heavier. We'll be slingshotting near the speed of light!"

"We'll be slinging out of control if we're not careful," Herman muttered. Too soon, they were in line for their first orbit. The corporal was already so far ahead that he looked very small on their screen.

"Turn it, turn it!" Sipoo cried, adjusting controls and hitting dials. *The Sun* arced wide as it came around. They were losing ground as the corporal got even farther ahead.

Herman brought them closer to the star as their orbit curved. The corporal's ship was almost out of sight. "He's so worried about leaving us in the dust, he's forgetting to tighten his slingshot," Sipoo observed. "What did you do to make him mad?"

"I think that was you," Herman retorted. Behind him, a circulation vent hissed urgently. It was starting to get hot in here.

"He's out of sight," Herman said after a moment. Sweat beaded on his forehead and hands. Sipoo removed her wig, flung it on the floor, and turned her attention to environment control.

"When the pit was the last time you had the air conditioning serviced?" she demanded suddenly. "It's not working well enough!"

"Space is a vast expanse of frozen nothing!" Herman snapped defensively. "Why would I worry about air conditioning?"

"If it gets too hot in here, you'll wish you had worried about it!" *The Sun* was shuddering under the stress. The grate on the ventilation vent rattled. "Tighten that arc! We don't have to be fast, just good."

"Pits, Sipoo, it's not every day I run my ship meters away from a star's outer sphere! I'm more worried about keeping us *warm* in space than cold most of the time!" While he was shouting, he obeyed his partner. The shuddering did not cease, but the ship's path tightened and they swerved away from the star. Now it was time for the slingshot portion of the game, when they turned and used the sheer force of their speed to dive back at the star.

Sipoo forgot about the air conditioning as she poured over the scanners. "Where is he? Where is he?" She slammed her fist on the counter. "This will never work if we lose him!"

"All we have to do is sling the closest to the sun! Who cares if we've lost him?"

"I care!" Sipoo shouted. Her feet were planted wide to keep from falling as *The Sun* twisted and turned wildly. The star's gravitation had already pulled them into a faster rate than they could normally achieve on their own. The back of Herman's nose felt pulled, as if he was leaving parts of himself behind.

The star came at them much faster than before. Herman

forced himself to focus strictly on guiding his ship into a new orbital path. Just in front of him, a small screen was spitting out thousands of panicked numbers as the ship's computer calculated temperature limits and meltdown times.

They managed to get a little closer that time. The temperature climbed noticeably. Herman shed his outer shirt and used it to wipe his brow. Although she was sweating, Sipoo refused to unbutton her jacket. She gathered her hair into a tight bun.

A bright plume of fire suddenly appeared on the edge of the screen. It glowed bright red and whitened as it grew. "Solar flare!" Sipoo roared. "Raise the pitch to positive 48 degrees!"

"It can't handle it!" Herman rejoined. "We need to hold it steady!"

"Do it!" Sipoo countered forcefully.

With misgivings, Herman obeyed. It was not often that she spoke to him like that, but sometimes she knew what she was talking about. Loose change and a coffee cup slid off of the counters and clattered on the floor as *The Sun* pointed its nose upwards. The flare was under them now, its massive heat and deadly radiation more of a danger than ever. "Push it!" Sipoo cried. "Push it to starboard! Maintain vertical pull!"

"Piiiiiits!" Herman yelled.

The ship veered to the right as it continued its upward climb. The solar flare arced gracefully and collided back into its birth mother. *The Sun* turned and went down, faster and faster until it looked like it would join the flare. The thruster array fired and pushed the ship into a near horizontal orbit with the massive giant.

"That was easy," Sipoo said.

"Sure," Herman muttered. He looked at his console. The burn on their fuel had taken up a sizeable amount. If they didn't slingshot again soon, there would not be another close call to talk about.

Sipoo eyed her reflection in one of the monitors. "How do I look?" she asked offhandedly. There was no way she was serious, but Herman whistled anyway. Ultrasound scans started to bleep, printing scattered readouts on their tiny screens.

"Moons, here he comes!" Sipoo excitedly bounced on her feet. She opened a side cabinet to reveal another scanner and control console. Hurriedly, she flipped switches.

"What the pit?" Herman half stood up. "Sipoo??"

"He's coming up on us from behind. He's in a hurry, too. I'll only have one chance at this. Monitor him, Herman! Don't let him get away!" Sipoo was already hailing him via telescreen. "This is *Dying Sun 009*. Do you copy? *Dying Sun 009* to Corporal Jones. Answer me, you self-serving excuse for bad company!"

"Sipoo, you can't be serious—"

"Corporal Jones, do you copy? This is *The Dying Sun 009*." Sipoo flipped a final switch and sat down with a satisfied sigh. A tiny screen at the bottom of the console came to life. Corporal Jones' ship was perfectly aligned in the middle of it.

"We're going to die," Herman said to himself. There was no one else that would listen to him. "Worse yet, we're not getting any money out of this. Sipoo?"

Even the crackle of static when the telescreen patched Corporal Jones through to them sounded smug. The man's lips were thin with victory, and his eyes were narrower than ever. "So, you wish to give up? I warned you. For a price, I might be willing to…" His voice trailed away when he saw Sipoo half-turned in her chair. His face changed as if he had suddenly recognized her. She wiggled her fingers in a friendly hello.

"Remember me?" she asked before hitting a solitary, rarely used, button.

Corporal Jones opened his mouth to shout as his eyes rounded in shock and indignation. "Sipoo-!" he cried. A sudden, purposeful explosion from the rear rattled the ship. Communications were cut abruptly. The telescreen filled with static.

"Outward view!" Sipoo cried exultantly. So filled with morbid fascination over what had just happened was he,

Herman was already turning the monitors over. The two of them watched wordlessly as the corporal's ship, crippled with one engine blasted, careened into the star. Sipoo breathed outward in obvious ecstasy. The ship vanished with an almost disappointing bright light.

Herman shook his head to himself and steered out of the star's orbit. Laughing so hard she could barely work the buttons, Sipoo unbuttoned her jacket. She was still laughing as they entered normal space. Sipoo continued to chuckle and gloat, occasionally bursting into new fits of laughter. It was like being trapped in a tin box with a madman. At least the temperature in the cabin was finally cooling to something more comfortable.

Suddenly, ship scans picked up something coming at them. "It's not over yet," Herman said. Sipoo laughed again. It was an expectant laugh he had heard before. He hated that laugh.

The referee ship had closed in on them from behind. Lights were blinking unremittingly. "Do I answer their call?"

"You're a racer, aren't you?" Sipoo challenged. There were genuine tears of joy in her eyes. "What have you always done in this sort of situation? Let's think about it. What would the other hoodlums do?"

Herman punched a few buttons, thinking about what he could possibly say to that woman. There was no way they could possibly pay whatever it was Corporal Jones had promised her. On the other hand, Herman's reputation was on the line (not to mention his plans for later). It was the referee's accepted place to open fire if she felt the game had been betrayed.

There was no doubt that Sipoo had betrayed the game. Purposefully disabling your opponent was a mortal sin to slingshotters everywhere. Many people who took slingshot racing very seriously were going to be angry. They would outnumber the other set of people who would be relieved that such fierce competition had been eliminated permanently.

"What the frag did he ever do to you?" Herman demanded of his partner. The lights were still blinking, but the referee was not going to wait forever. Sooner or later, she was going to open fire.

"He didn't die the last time I tried to kill him," Sipoo said. She habitually touched her earpiece. "So, what are we going to do here? Do you want to talk to her or not?" Sipoo sounded more amused than irritated, even though she was no longer laughing.

Herman's finger hovered over the connect switch. "What did you bet on this race, anyway? How much of a cut is this woman going to expect?"

Sipoo smoothly buckled herself into her chair before saying, "To be quite honest, I bet him enough money to buy two small moons. Also and for the record, this woman you're so worried about happens to be his niece. She probably hasn't blown us to Sundry and Come yet because of the money."

Herman made his decision and flipped another, rarely used switch at the bottom of his console. *Dying Sun 009* opened its auxiliary thrusts and flared into motion. Sipoo laughed as her investments spurred them out of reach. There was a single shot that shook them before the star was a rapidly shrinking dot in the distance. Even as other stars began to come close, Sipoo was still chortling.

"You're going to kill us with your little vendettas one of these days," Herman said after chewing his lip in silent frustration. "Someone is going to come after you."

"If I don't get them first," she chirruped. "I'm up for some wine. Want some?"

"So long as it's not water," Herman said, adjusting controls and enjoying the vast cold of deep space.

ETERNAL

He stood in their bathroom with the door open, picking at his belly. He thought she was asleep.

From where she lay on their modest bed, she could see the angle of his torso and the strength in his thighs. She wanted to rub her hands on his chest and lay her cheek there. He towered over her during those times and wrapped his arms around her like she was a fragile package. The embrace was all she felt she would ever need.

He turned his head. "I thought you were asleep," he said, coming out of the bathroom to stand by the bed. "When did you get up?"

"When you did," she replied sitting up. The blanket fell from her upper body to reveal her naked bosom. "Don't go."

"Okay," he said with a smile. "But after two weeks the checks will stop coming. Then the MP's will come to the door looking for me."

"We'll run away," she said. "We'll go to Canada."

"I doubt they'd let you in."

"Germany, then."

"How will we get there?"

He crawled on the bed to hover his body over hers. With one hand he pushed her down, and then he smothered her in a kiss. She arched into his embrace and nibbled his neck. His hands slid to her buttocks.

In this way they made love the way they had always done, since the first time ages ago. They took it slow and, once finished, held each other tightly despite the sweat on their skin. It was he that finally pushed her away, gently.

"Our anniversary is this Friday," he said. "Our first. I never thought we'd come this far."

"I never thought I'd see you again," she said. "I wish you didn't have to go."

"You know I have to."

"Yeah."

He got up, then, and put on his clothes. He would be walking out the door soon to board a flight and return to his unit in Iraq. It was something he had done before in other wars, she knew. It was something she had done to him as well. The knowledge was not enough to make her feel any better.

She got up suddenly and grabbed him, burying her face into his back and sobbing. He turned, peeling her off, to cup her face in his hands.

"I'm coming back," he said.

"You always say that," she said, wiping a tear away. "Sometimes it never happens."

"But I'm here now," he reasoned. "To be here I had to come back, right?"

She looked at the floor.

To be here he had to come back. It took him a lifetime, and now she was someone new. She thought she would never see him again. Failed relationship after failed relationship had left her resigned that her memories would interfere with living in the now always. Then he came back, hardly remembering who he was but himself just the same. Personality quirks she had joked about to friends suddenly returned to life. He had come back to life.

It would be easier, she thought, if he remembered something. Anything. She never talked to him about their mutual past. With past life recollection, there were many unspoken taboos. Feeding someone memories they did not recall was one of them. You did not tamper nor play with another person's mind.

There were times he doubted who he was, but she knew. She believed. The coincidences were too stacked to be just that, and there was but one soul in the cosmos who touched her the way he did. There was but one.

She thought of a secure place a long time ago when they, newlywed, wrapped themselves in furs and covered their faces with their own wings. Her heart always went to that moment. It was romantic, soft, made tender by the stretch of memory. It was the moment "they" began.

She followed him to the kitchen and watched him make an egg sandwich. He was taking his time with everything that morning. He always did that when he had to go away.

He made her an egg sandwich, too.

They ate together on the porch in silence. The neighbor's dog wandered into the backyard. She threw it her bread crusts, which it caught out of mid-air, and she licked her fingers. He watched her, smiling.

"What?"

"You're just like a big kid."

"Look who's talking. Card game, anyone?"

"I have to keep up with you somehow."

"I doubt that."

His sandwich finished, he went inside. She took the dirty plates to wash them. He poured himself a glass of juice and drank it in one gulp.

There was a day, she half-remembered, when she stood at another sink with her apron tied around her waist washing dishes. She thought it might have been June or July. Their children were outside playing with the neighborhood bunch. She could hear them in the background over the hum of their little refrigerator. Or maybe it had been a fan. The memory was not clear enough to be able to tell.

She had been thinking about the way he chuckled at her jokes when there was a knock on the door.

"Mrs—" She could not remember her name from back then. She never could remember names. "Ma'am, we regret to inform you…."

Tears sprang to her eyes and her heart clenched. She nearly dropped the dish she was holding. Her husband moved in the other room, gathering his belongings and stuffing his duffel bag. Outside the neighbor's children had just emerged to play basketball in the cul de sac. She could hear them in the background.

There was another time, she remembered involuntarily, when the Church put their land on loan and sent him to the other side of the world. She stayed behind because she had to, but given a choice she would have followed. He never came home again. She wasn't sure if she lost the land. All she could recall was that lost feeling as she stood at the window to her room, looking out at the countryside.

It wasn't truly the other side of the world back then. That was back then. Now it really was the other side of the world, and he was going to the same place as before. How many more bodies did those sands have to claim before it was finally over?

With a hand towel, she dried the two dishes and forced herself to think of something else. The most romantic thing he had done ever, she decided, was to draw a heart on the car window. She had been sitting in the cab. He walked up to the car, fogged the window with his breath, and drew the heart while smiling at her.

There was a step to her left. She clenched her hands together and turned around. She had to wear a brave face. This wasn't Vietnam. It wasn't the War of the Roses nor a Crusade. Soldiers did not ride horses nor carry clubs. He was safer than the other times, she told herself.

"Time to go," he said. "My ride is here."

"I know." She bit her lip.

He slung his duffel bag over his shoulder and kissed her on the mouth. "I'll be back," he reassured her again. She did not answer even as he turned to go. She followed him to the door.

He paused at the door with the morning sunlight filtering around him. Placing his hand on her head, he said, "Our anniversary is this Friday."

"Our first," she said, trying to smile.

His eyes flicked up above her head as he looked at something far away. "Maybe," he said. "But I do remember something about that. There were candles in a cavern. Someone had piled furs into, I don't know. It was like a natural outcropping shaped like a bowl. It was very soft and warm. Kind of like a nest, you know. You were there wearing this white shimmery gauze thing. At least I'm pretty sure it was you."

Casually his gaze returned to the present and her face. "Anyway, I'll be back. My unit is supposed to leave Iraq in four months, and then I'll be back in the States. You'll probably get sick of me inside a week."

"I doubt that," she said. "I haven't gotten tired of you yet, have I?"

"You only want me for the money."

"I thought it was the great sex."

They kissed again. His kiss was hard as always, but she welcomed it. "Happy anniversary," he said. "Our first anniversary."

"Or ten thousandth," she said. "I stopped counting ages ago."

She watched him get into the taxi from the front door and stood there until the car was out of sight. She cried a little bit to herself before going back inside. Then came a wave of relief. She curled onto the couch and stared at the blank screen of the TV.

He would be back, she told herself. And she knew he always would.

FAMILY TRIP

Prehistory

The clan mothers of the Fang-Toe Clan had just grabbed their share of the kill when the sky split with the sound of thunder. A blinding white light illuminated everything, accenting the gaunt primates' faces. Everyone scattered, screaming, into the forest. Their screams chased behind, reverberating from the rocky mountain sides. Then as suddenly as it had appeared, it stopped. The light vanished.

Tall Weaver, the wisest of the clan mothers, picked her way from the woods, stood in awe of the burned ground where their camp had been. Behind her, the rest of the clan timidly edged forward. She turned.

"The gods are angry," she cried, tossing the meat from her. "I told you the white spear horn was sacred! We've been punished for killing it!"

As one mass, the clan fell on their knees to beg forgiveness.

1959

The mountains were older, rounded, and covered with forest. William Stark knew every inch of them. He had walked them for pleasure as an adolescent and to cut them during the Depression. This time, he was waiting to die. He had felt it coming for many weeks now.

The far off sound of thunder warned him of rain. Shrugging his bony shoulders, he started packing his cooking gear. After he was gone, it could rust all it wanted. Right now, he needed it.

The thunder transformed into a loud rumbling. A shadow chilled William's backside. He looked up.

"Excuse me," cried a friendly voice. "But, could I trouble you for the time?"

"E-eh ... eleven-thirty," William stammered.

"No, man! The year!"

"1959," William managed.

"Thanks!" the voice shouted. The shadow streaked away, carrying William's visitor with it.

Aliens. William had just been visited by aliens.

He recovered his breath, packed his gear, and hiked home. He told his story to the first government agent he found—a secretary who listened with a puzzled expression—and went to church. He died of heart failure ten years later while at the pulpit.

866

Little Man made his way silently through the brush, pushing branches carefully out of his way. He looked at the sun, then wished he had not. It was lunchtime, and he was very hungry.

This was only the second day of what he privately called, "The Starving Walk." Actually, he was on a vision quest. He had prepared for it by entering the sweat lodge in the evening, and walking out again in the morning. He would not eat until his vision came.

His brothers had said no vision would come to him. He could not even think of the task with a respectful attitude, how could he expect the spirits to bless him with a vision? Still, Little Man went and walked. He would not go back until he succeeded.

Something ripped through the sky above him. Little Man dove for cover, although it felt like he'd left his heart and bowels behind. Above him, the trees swayed and cracked. Branches showered down around him.

"Bloody hellfire!" a voice shouted in English. Of course, Little Man did not speak English and had never heard the language before in his life. He poked his head out from cover just enough to see what was going on.

A gigantic silver bird—a thunderbird!—churned the ground beneath it before launching upward. More branches broke and fell heavily. Little Man did not even wince as he watched the bird fly away. He was so awed by the sight, he stood in the naked open with his mouth agape.

His brothers could say nothing now that he had seen the thunderbird for his vision! Little Man lightly leaped through the mess and headed for home.

By now, the ship's inhabitants had lost all track of when they were.

The sky split one final time, spitting the camper shuttle into a pocket of turbulence. The shuttle shuddered violently, flew smoothly as the onboard computer adjusted internal settings, and circled for a landing. This time, there was a convenient clearing available. The machine came to a rest.

"Damn!" cried the familiar voice as the owner looked outside again. The owner, a dark man of average height, climbed outside and made way to the engine case. He knocked the door open violently and looked inside.

"What's wrong with it, Davey?" a woman called from behind. Followed by three children of various ages, she scrambled to the ground and gratefully stretched.

"The timing ring is corrupted," the man said with feeling. "We're stuck here until the rental company finds us."

The woman looked around at the forming glaciers and wild untamed countryside. When her husband had suggested a family trip to the Yellowstone International Park, she had assumed that meant on the correct time line.

"Mommy, I have to go to the bathroom," whined their youngest, squeezing her legs together.

Somewhere at the foot of a nearby mountain someone lit a fire, all set to do what it took to appease a god.

STUMBLING THROUGH THE DARK

I was about 16 when I wrote this story: back when Dungeons and Dragons was new and Magic the Gathering was but a twinkle in a god's eye. Other folks have made these jokes since then, so this tale is hardly original.

Four blazing torches pervaded their light across the threatening dark of the ancient dungeon. It, the dungeon, had been carved by unmentioned hands at great labor and expense. Bones littered the aisles. Carved warnings in forgotten languages were everywhere like insane stucco.

Two humans, a dwarf and two elves rushed their way up a slimy stairway. One almost stumbled, but he was saved by luck and managed to keep running. They only paused once, to look behind themselves. The roar of pursuit pushed them forward, bursting out at the top of the stair and stopping short.

Zombies shambled forward from a few feet away. Their teeth showed through rotting orifices in their flesh in a grinning mockery. They paused and one scratched its head in apparent thought before resuming its stance.

The dwarf boldly stepped forward, brandishing a deadly-looking battle axe. Its name was Burger Slicer, and it was blessed by the god Hammerfell with a curious taste for rotting flesh. It was stained with decay from previous excursions.

As the zombies waited for their turn, one of the humans stepped to the dwarf's side. She was young (all adventurers tend to start out that way) and dressed in strange plate mail. No self respecting smith would have designed such ill-suited armor; neither would a barbarian be caught dead in it.

Or rather, the barbarian would be caught dead in it. That was the problem. The mail barely covered the most tender parts of the woman's anatomy and none whatsoever of anything else.

"I'm getting tired of this."

She imperiously shoved the dwarf behind her and held up a strange symbol on a chain. The zombies seemed to struggle for a moment – long enough to throw a pairof dice —then almost regretfully turned and retreated. The woman stashed her symbol somewhere unfathomable and turned meaningfully to her company.

"Let's go," she said, gesturing to the black stairway for emphasis. Scuffling sounds sounded from below were growing louder. The group ran from the stairway, taking a westward passage.

"I thought I was the leader," one of the other humans complained loudly. In the rush, he had been jostled just behind the woman.

"Whatever, Greg," the woman sighed. Everyone stopped running to rearrange themselves. Greg retook his position in the front. Everyone else placed themselves one by one in a neat row with the dwarf at the end.

"I'm tired of being placed last," the dwarf whined. "I get too many swipes by ambushing monsters."

With this in mind, the group rearranged themselves again. This time, one of the elves was last. He shrugged his slight shoulders while fingering his mighty bow, Hawthorn.

"My life is low," he said. "But I can take a few more hits. When do we stop to rest and heal?"

"When we find someplace safe," the woman in the scant armor said. "By rights, the pursuit should have caught us by now. Can we please?" She pointed down the passageway.

The group dashed down the hall as if they never had stopped. Before long, they came to a fork in the path.

"This way," said the youngest elf. Named Jenny, her black hair hung disheveled about her face. Then again, it always did. Even after brushing. Her friends were so used to her wild appearance they could not imagine her any other way. So even here that's how she was. Anything else would have seemed unnatural.

"Could you try to give me a little credit?" Jenny said defensively. "I try."

"What are you talking about?" Cliff, the dwarf, asked impatiently. "We haven't even argued about the way yet."

"Well," Jenny said, "you were going to do that, too. But, that's enough cracks about my hair. I'm tired of it."

"Well, I'm tired of zombies every time we turn around," the dwarf grunted. "Cindy keeps chasing them away before I can gain experience-—"

"Helloh-oh," Cindy said. "Do you hear that?"

"What?" everyone asked, listening.

"The sounds of pursuit, coming down the hall?" the woman suggested hopefully.

"Oh." Then everyone did hear it. They nodded enthusiastically and turned back to Jenny.

"This way," she said helpfully. Her eyes glittered feverishly in the torchlight as she examined the intricately carved walls and noticed the hint of fresh air. "Good description, Joshua. I like that. This is the way out."

Greg considered, shifting his backpack. "Then this is the way to go."

"Suppose it's still booby trapped?" asked the wounded elf, whose name was something fancy like Sir Elverand

D'ilbraharrad Soothsayer. Nobody could remember it, not even him, so they just called him Paul. Taking chances never was a favorite pastime of his, and now he had incentive not to.

"I will cast a detect-trap spell," said Cindy.

"Not enough time," said Greg. "We must take the chance."

"It will only take——"

"No."

"Aw." The woman scuffed the ground with a sandaled foot but acceded. The group lined themselves up for another run.

"No time now!" someone cried.

Behind them, wall to wall skeletons marched in military fashion.

"Christ!" Cindy swore, taking measures to run in the opposite direction whether she was followed or not. The others fell into step behind, regardless of order.

Suddenly, Jenny faltered in her light steps.

"Wait a minute," she said. The others stopped running and gathered around her. She turned to the woman. "Cindy, I thought you worshiped Aphrodite."

"You're not gonna start that again, are you?!?" Cindy nearly screamed. Her eyes darted nervously behind them. The skeletal army was catching up quickly.

"Oh, are you gonna play or not?" Greg asked in frustration. "Joshua has explained it I don't know how many times——"

"I'm sorry, I guess I don't understand this game," the little elf said abashedly. "I thought, you know, each person was supposed to stick to their character. And Cindy is supposed to be a barbaric priestess of Aphrodite's Blue Cult."

"Just run for it!"

"Too late!" someone cried.

The group, miraculously surrounded by menacing skeletons, huddled together in a circle.

"Can't your symbol do anything?" cried the youngest elf.

"No!" Cindy cried, hoping they would be allowed first attack. The numbers were overwhelming. She was sure they were going to die. "I can only do it once a day. I've already used it, remember?"

The first skeleton attacked Cindy before she could bring her sword, Shinebright, to bear. Cindy rolled out of the way, and the skeleton missed. The other skeletons immediately attacked, one by one in neat order.

The dwarf swung his halberd, striking a skeleton. It shattered in a cloud of dust. Some of the dust got into Cindy's eyes, although she was on the far side of the circle. She coughed, out for at least the time one skeleton could attack four times.

"Oh stop, stop," Cindy said despairingly. The wounded

elf went down with a cry from a nasty blow across the neck. "Great, now Paul is dead. Stop!"

Like an order from above, everything did stop, melting away as each brought their imaginations back under control. Joshua picked up the dice from the table.

"Sorry, guys," Cindy said, gathering up her papers. "I'm late for work. I knew there wouldn't be time to get far in this game."

"I'm dead anyway," Paul said with an easy shrug. He was already rolling up a new character, shaking his head at the stats.

"But can't we work some magic or something and bring your character back?" Jenny asked. "Gosh, isn't this game supposed to be about stuff like that?"

"Not with Joshua over there as game coordinator," Greg muttered.

"That doesn't seem very fair," Jenny said.

"Life is never fair," Joshua said ominously. "And neither are the games we play."

"Oh come off it," Cindy barked. "And go start your car. I've gotta go. Are you guys coming with me? I'll buy you a pizza to munch while I wait on the customers."

"Great!" Cliff said, rubbing his hands together happily. He could swing into a pizza like an axe cutting butter.

The young adventurers put away their dungeon, folding it neatly and tucking it into a blue folder. It, the dungeon, had been created at great expense. The drafter's paper, which Joshua had insisted upon, had cost Cindy one night's tips. The rest was just India ink, blotting places like insane stucco where Greg had carelessly shaken his special pens.

THE FICTION WORKSHOP FINAL

Even though I was going to school to be an anthropologist, I took a fiction writing workshop one semester. This little piece was written as a final requirement: you chose your grade. If my instructor felt you did a real good job, you got an A. But otherwise it was implied you got the grade you thought you deserved...

Blue sat back in her chair, eyed the confusing syllabus for the hundredth time that semester, and breathed, "Dear gods." Once again, she read the paper.

> <u>Final</u>: **Pass/Fail. You cannot complete the course with a passing grade unless you hand in the following:**
>
> An assessment of your own endeavors during the term, including a statement of the grade you believe you deserve (not the grade you would like) and why. This assessment can be academic/argumentative or creative. Again, I'm open to your ideas. You get extra

credit if is both well-done AND funny.

Right! As if she could be funny past a pounding head-ache, a looming traffic ticket, and the antics of her room-mate/former-pastlife-nanna! What on earth could she pos-sibly do to be amusing to the man who has read it all? This was prose she had to write; not one of her three panel com-ics or splash panel sarcasms. This was the real thing with real words!

Anyway, dammit, she thought that school bus was broke down when she passed it. Usually, busses don't pull up on the sidewalk when stopped. Nor do they refrain from putting out their little stop sign. The cop had been under-standing enough, and even suggested she could fight the ticket. But, then she would have to go through the drama of going to court! Last she checked, she did not care much for kangaroos.

At least he had been cute.

Well, the assignment seemed easy enough. All she had to do was tell Ari (as he liked to be called, although her mental description leaned more towards "Bushy Eyebrows with High Vibrations") what grade she felt she deserved. It seemed easy enough.

Okay, it wasn't as easy as it sounded.

In desperation, Blue turned to her mental congress to debate the matter. Kat lounged on the "visual couch" to watch the world go by. The couch was set, as usual, right behind Blue's eyes so that Kat could watch events like normal people would a television. She had a box of chocolates and three calendar boys. Blue breathed a sigh of relief.

Within the great space that was Blue's mind, she was just a voice that spoke through surround sound speakers in the corners. Kat was the entity that resided here. She called the place her "flat." This was usually a good working arrangement, but Blue still shuddered at the one time she looked into the flat and saw Kat with—

Anyway, Blue posed the problem to Kat who slipped a chocolate covered cherry into her mouth. The feline-woman's canines popped the desert audibly. Blue winced. That was just plain nasty.

"Of course you deserve the highest grade in the class," Kat observed. "Aren't we the cleverest person in the room? And the prettiest?"

If Blue had arms in Kat's world, she would have smacked the feline. "No, you just think that. Most writers think something along those lines. Anyway, the highest grade in the class might not be so high if the others did not do so well. And I'm not so sure I deserve the highest grade."

Kat feigned insult and shock. "Why ever not?" she asked in her thick southern accent. She flicked her striped tail. A field of white mist drifted into Blue's view, and before she knew it the flat was no longer accessible. There would be no help there.

Damn damn triple damn damn. Okay, she would just have to be honest to herself. And the truth was that being sick had gotten in the way of her scholastic progress. No, she didn't mean the presence of Kat, the flat, or a nanny from several centuries ago. She was referring to when she allowed acute bronchitis to feed her natural affinity towards sleeping.

Blue loved to sleep.

Overall, the assignments in the class could have been done from a death bed. And did she do them? Did she take a moment from sleeping or smoking cigarettes to print a page, lean back on the pillow, and read? No. She slept. And when she was feeling better, she still slept when she had the chance. So, as much as she hated to admit it to herself, on an alphabetical scale, she deserved an A+ for being lazy and a C for her fiction workshop class.

And that was the truth, and she could not deny it. Well, Blue consoled herself, a C is much better than an F. For one thing, it's a much prettier and useful shape. If you put a C on it's side, it looked kind of like a cup.

"You can drink vodka from cups," Kat suggested from nowhere.

And besides, Blue could remember when she was a C

cup. It was much better than this tragic D and a half cup she was forced to endure day after day. Going underwear shopping was horrible. Don't clothing designers realize that Blue was put on this earth just to be served?! Why, there should be an entire line of half-sized bras just for her, readily accessible in any clothing store.

And they should be free, too. Because Blue was meant to be served. And allowed to sleep.

"See? That wasn't so hard," Kat said. "You just wrote your final."

Placing cigarette to lips without inhaling, Blue scanned the work for errors. There were grammatical ones, she was sure… but she couldn't find any aside from the intentionally placed ones. Alright, then. There was her paper.

"It seems slightly anticlimactic though," Blue commented to herself. "I mean, it just sort of ends."

"I think it depends on where you're looking," Kat said before grabbing one of her boys and shutting the windows to the flat.

ABOUT THE AUTHOR

K. J. Joyner comes from a culture where storytellers are very special, so she was encouraged to write for most of her life with gifts of typewriters, magazines, and long-distance contact with famous people. She wishes she could earn the money to travel, but if wishes were horses she'd ride where she wants to go practically free.

OTHER WORK BY K. J. JOYNER

Comics and Prose

A Bird in a Bush (webcomic)
Battle of Angels
Beloved (webcomic)
Black Wolf, Silver Fox
Moon Balloon
Life of Death
There's Nothing Romantic About Washing the Dishes
-ologist at LARGE
Whimsical Words and Dramatic Affairs—A Book of Badly Written Poetry
Only the Innocent
Going Under
Heavenly Bride
The Page of Cups (with Tim Belcher)

If She Only Had a Brain

The Future of Powwow Dancing in Native America
Cycles of Change: A Look at Global Warming